ORDINARY BY LOOKS, EXTRAORDINARY BY HEART : WILL YOU BE MY FOREVER?

A LOVE BEYOND LOOK

MANOJ YADAV

To all the dreamers and believers,

This book is dedicated to those who see beyond the surface, who recognize the extraordinary within the ordinary. May you always embrace your true self and find the beauty in every heart you encounter.

To my family and friends,
your unwavering support and encouragement have been my guiding light.
Thank you for believing in my dreams.

And to everyone who has ever felt overlooked,
remember that your heart is your greatest asset. Let it shine brightly, for love knows no bounds.

Contents

Contents

Contents

Foreword

In a world often captivated by external appearances, it is a profound journey to delve into the essence of true beauty—the beauty of the heart. **Ordinary by Looks, Extraordinary by Heart: Will You Be My Forever?** invites readers to explore the intricate tapestry of love, friendship, and self-discovery.

This story, set against the backdrop of everyday life, captures the struggles and triumphs of Kartik and Arushi, two individuals whose paths intertwine in unexpected ways. As we follow their journey, we are reminded that love transcends superficial judgments and that it is the depth of our character that defines us.

Through relatable characters, heartfelt dialogues, and emotional nuances, the narrative encourages us to embrace our authenticity. It highlights the importance of self-acceptance and the courage to love oneself before seeking love from others. The story also emphasizes the value of true connections—those built on trust, kindness, and understanding.

As you turn these pages, may you find reflections of your own experiences, dreams, and aspirations. May the journey of Kartik and Arushi inspire you to look beyond appearances and recognize the extraordinary qualities that lie within each of us.

Thank you for joining us on this beautiful adventure of love and self-discovery.

— [Manoj Yadav]

Preface

As I sit down to pen the preface for **Ordinary by Looks, Extraordinary by Heart: Will You Be My Forever?**, I am filled with a sense of gratitude and excitement. This story is not just a tale of love; it is a reflection of the myriad emotions, struggles, and triumphs that we all encounter in our lives.

In a society that often equates worth with appearances, I felt compelled to write about the beauty that lies beneath the surface—the beauty that is often overlooked. This narrative follows the journey of Kartik and Arushi, two characters whose experiences mirror the essence of what it means to love and be loved. Their story unfolds against the backdrop of everyday challenges, reminding us that love is not merely a fairytale but a profound connection that can change our lives in unexpected ways.

Through their eyes, we explore themes of self-acceptance, the power of friendship, and the transformative nature of love. Kartik, an unassuming hero, teaches us that true strength comes from kindness and emotional depth. Arushi, with her vibrant spirit, embodies the courage to see beyond the surface and appreciate the heart of another.

As you embark on this journey with them, I hope you find inspiration in their experiences and reflect on the importance of looking beyond appearances. May you be encouraged to embrace your uniqueness and recognize the extraordinary qualities within yourself and others.

Thank you for allowing me to share this story with you. It is my hope that it resonates with your heart and inspires you to seek and celebrate the beauty within.

Acknowledgements

Writing a book is a journey that cannot be undertaken alone, and I am deeply grateful to all those who have supported me throughout this process.

First and foremost, I would like to express my heartfelt appreciation to my family. Your unwavering belief in my dreams and your constant encouragement have been my greatest motivation. To my parents, thank you for instilling in me the values of hard work and perseverance.

A special thank you to my mentor, whose guidance and wisdom have been invaluable in refining my writing and enhancing my storytelling skills. Your faith in my abilities pushed me to dig deeper and explore the themes that matter most.

To my readers, thank you for taking the time to immerse yourselves in Kartik and Arushi's journey. Your willingness to explore the depths of love and connection alongside them makes all the effort worthwhile.

Lastly, I would like to acknowledge the countless authors, both classic and contemporary, who have paved the way for storytellers like me. Your work has inspired me to find my own voice and share my stories with the world.

This book is a reflection of all the love, support, and encouragement I have received along the way. I hope it resonates with you and inspires you to recognize the extraordinary beauty within yourself and those around you.

— [Manoj Yadav]

Prologue

In a world where appearances often dictate perceptions, the true essence of a person can be overshadowed by the fleeting allure of external beauty. This is a story that delves into the hearts of two seemingly ordinary individuals—Kartik and Arushi—who navigate the complexities of love, friendship, and self-discovery in the backdrop of their professional lives.

Kartik, an introverted engineer, carries the weight of self-doubt, often believing that his simple looks overshadow the kindness and compassion that reside within him. Arushi, a spirited and ambitious woman, is adored by many but yearns for a connection that goes beyond the superficial. As their paths cross in the corporate jungle, they find themselves drawn to one another, igniting a friendship that challenges their perceptions of love and worth.

Through laughter and tears, triumphs and setbacks, Kartik and Arushi's journey unfolds, revealing the transformative power of love that lies beneath the surface. They are joined by their loyal friends, Aniket and Meera, who play pivotal roles in guiding them towards self-acceptance and deeper understanding.

This narrative serves as a reminder that true beauty is not defined by how one looks but by the love, kindness, and authenticity that emanates from within. As you embark on this journey with Kartik and Arushi, may you discover that the heart's whisper is louder than the world's judgment and that sometimes, it takes the ordinary to reveal the extraordinary.

Welcome to a tale of love that transcends appearances and resonates in the depths of the heart—a story that promises to challenge your perspectives and inspire you to embrace your own extraordinary self.

CHAPTER ONE

The Invisible Man

(Kartik's Office Desk – Morning)

Kartik is typing on his computer, focused on fixing a system issue. People walk by, chatting, but no one stops to talk to him.

Aniket (walking past):

"Morning, bro. Same old grind, huh?"

Kartik (smiles slightly, not looking up):

"Yeah, nothing new. Just trying to keep things running."

Aniket shrugs and continues walking, leaving Kartik in his world of quiet work.

(Suddenly, Arushi walks over, her presence catching Kartik off guard.)

Arushi (cheerfully):

"Kartik, right?"

Kartik freezes for a second, then looks up at her, unsure how to respond.

Kartik (clears his throat):

"Uh, yeah. That's me."

Arushi (smiling):

"I heard you're the go-to guy when something breaks around here. Mind helping me with my system? It's acting up, and I have no idea what's going on."

Kartik stands up quickly, a bit awkwardly, nodding.

Kartik (nervous):

"Sure. What's the problem?"

They walk over to her desk. Kartik starts looking at the screen while Arushi stands beside him.

Arushi (leaning in slightly, watching):
"Honestly, this thing hates me. It's frozen three times today. You'd think with all this tech, it would just work."

Kartik smiles slightly, focusing on the issue, his fingers flying over the keyboard. After a moment, the screen refreshes, and the problem is solved.

Kartik:
"It was just a memory overload. Should be fine now."

Arushi (impressed):
"Wow, that was fast! You're like a magician with these things."

Kartik scratches his head, a bit shy.

Kartik:
"Not really. Just... something I've done a lot."

Arushi (grinning):
"Well, you definitely saved me. Thanks, Kartik. I owe you one."

Kartik nods, still unsure how to respond, and heads back to his desk. Arushi watches him go, a curious expression on her face.

(Kartik's Desk – Later that Day)
Kartik sits quietly, thinking about the interaction with Arushi. His thoughts are interrupted by Aniket's return.

Aniket (teasing):
"Saw you talking to Arushi! What was that about?"

Kartik looks up, flustered.

Kartik:
"Nothing, man. She just needed help with her system."

Aniket (smirking):
"Sure, sure. Just work stuff, huh? Anyway, don't overthink it. She probably just likes your skills."

Kartik shrugs, looking back at his screen, but a small smile plays on his lips.*

Kartik (muttering):
"Yeah, maybe."

(Later – Lunch Break)

In the cafeteria, Kartik sits at a table alone, his meal untouched. He watches as groups of colleagues laugh and share stories. The atmosphere is vibrant, and he feels a twinge of longing. Just then, he spots Arushi entering with her lunch tray.

Arushi (looking around):
"Mind if I join you?"

Kartik blinks, a bit surprised but nods enthusiastically.

Kartik:
"Sure! I mean, if you want."

Arushi sits down, her tray clattering slightly as she sets it down.

Arushi:
"Great! So, tell me—what do you like to do outside of work? Any hobbies?"

Kartik hesitates, unsure of how much to share.

Kartik:
"Um, I like reading... and tinkering with tech stuff, I guess."

Arushi (leaning in):
"Tinkering? Like fixing things? You're a tech wizard at work and a wizard at home, too?"

Kartik chuckles, feeling more at ease.

Kartik:
"Something like that. I like figuring out how things work."

Arushi:
"That's cool! I wish I could fix things. I usually just break them."

Kartik laughs, imagining her struggling with tech.

Kartik:
"Well, I could give you some tips. But you'd have to promise not to break anything while I'm around."

They share a laugh, and Kartik feels the weight of his shyness lifting, replaced by a budding friendship.

Arushi:

"Deal! So, what are you reading right now?"

Kartik perks up, excited to talk about his current book.

Kartik:

"It's a mystery novel. I love trying to solve the puzzle before the characters do."

Arushi (intrigued):

"Nice! I'm more of a romantic novel fan myself. Can't resist a good love story."

Kartik raises an eyebrow, playful.

Kartik:

"Do you swoon over the characters?"

Arushi (laughs):

"Maybe a little! But I also love the drama and twists. Makes you feel alive."

Kartik watches her, intrigued by her passion, realizing how easy it is to talk to her. Their conversation flows effortlessly, filled with laughter and shared interests.

CHAPTER TWO

Breaking the Ice

(The Following Week – Morning)

The office is bustling with energy as everyone prepares for a big project. Kartik sits at his desk, reviewing his tasks when Arushi approaches again, looking excited.

Arushi:

"Kartik! I've got an idea for the project. Can we talk?"

Kartik looks up, intrigued, and nods eagerly.

Kartik:

"Of course! What's on your mind?"

They move to a quieter corner, where Arushi pulls out a notepad filled with ideas.

Arushi (enthusiastically):

"So, I was thinking we could incorporate some interactive elements into the campaign. Maybe a quiz or a poll to engage our audience more?"

Kartik leans in, analyzing her notes with genuine interest.

Kartik:

"That sounds great! Interactive content can really boost engagement. I could help with the technical setup."

Arushi (beaming):

"Yes! I knew you'd get it! Together, we can make this really dynamic."

Kartik feels a thrill at her enthusiasm and the collaborative spirit between them. As they discuss more ideas, the connection grows stronger.

(Later in the Week – Office Conference Room)

They gather with a small team to present their ideas. Arushi leads the presentation, exuding confidence. Kartik watches her, admiration growing as she speaks passionately about their concept.

Arushi:

"And with Kartik's tech expertise, we can ensure everything runs smoothly."

When it's Kartik's turn, he stands up, feeling nervous but encouraged by Arushi's supportive gaze.

Kartik:

"Uh, we've designed a few prototypes to showcase how the interactive elements will function..."

As he explains, he glances at Arushi, who nods approvingly. Slowly, he finds his voice and gains confidence.

Kartik:

"...and we believe this approach will not only engage our audience but also provide valuable feedback."

The team responds positively, and Kartik feels a rush of pride. When the meeting concludes, Arushi high-fives him.

Arushi:

"You were amazing! See? You just needed to believe in yourself."

Kartik smiles widely, the compliment lighting up his day.

Kartik:

"Thanks! I owe it to you for pushing me to share my ideas."

(After Work – Outside the Office)

As they leave the office together, Arushi turns to Kartik.

Arushi:

"How about we grab some coffee? Celebrate our success?"

Kartik feels a flutter of excitement, but also apprehension. He hesitates, but then nods.

Kartik:
"Sure! I'd like that."

They walk to a nearby café, chatting comfortably about their favorite drinks and stories from their lives. Kartik opens up more than he ever has, sharing anecdotes about his family and childhood, laughing at the memories.

Kartik:
"And then my brother tried to build a rocket. Let's just say it didn't go as planned."

Arushi (giggling):
"Oh no! What happened?"

Kartik recounts the details, his voice animated as he brings her into the story. He feels lighter, enjoying the laughter that flows between them. For the first time in a long while, he feels like he truly belongs.

(The Café – Evening)

As they finish their coffee, Kartik feels an unexplainable connection with Arushi. She glances at him, her eyes sparkling with curiosity.

Arushi:
"What about you? What's your dream? I mean, aside from fixing tech?"

Kartik takes a moment, contemplating her question.

Kartik:
"I guess I want to create something meaningful. Something that helps people, you know?"

Arushi watches him, her expression turning serious.

Arushi:
"I think you can definitely do that. You have a gift for understanding how things work. You could be a real force for good."

Kartik blushes at her praise, feeling a mix of pride and humility.

Kartik:
"Thanks, Arushi. That means a lot coming from you."

As they leave the café, the sun sets behind them, casting a warm glow. The air is filled with a sense of promise, and Kartik can't help but feel that this is the beginning of something special.

(Later – Kartik's Apartment)

Kartik sits on his couch, reflecting on the day. He feels lighter, as if a weight has been lifted. He pulls out his journal and begins to write.

Kartik (writing):

"Today was different. Today, I felt seen. Arushi has a way of breaking through my walls..."

He pauses, smiling to himself as he recalls her laughter and warmth. It's the first time he feels hopeful about friendship—and maybe even more.

CHAPTER THREE

Unseen Bonds

(The Office – Morning)

Kartik walks into the office the next day, feeling an unusual sense of anticipation. His thoughts keep drifting back to the conversation with Arushi at the café. For the first time in a long while, he feels genuinely excited about something more than work.

As he settles into his seat, he's greeted by an unexpected message on his phone.

Arushi's Message:

"Hey, Kartik! Got any plans for lunch today? Thinking about grabbing something different. Wanna join?"

Kartik stares at the message for a moment, caught off guard. His mind races—should he say yes? But before he can overthink, his fingers type a response.

Kartik's Reply:

"Sounds good! Let's do it."

He sends the message before he can second-guess himself. A moment later, Arushi replies with a thumbs-up emoji.

(The Office – Midday)

As lunchtime approaches, Kartik gathers his things and stands up just as Arushi approaches his desk, a wide grin on her face.

Arushi (cheerfully):

"Ready to go? I found this cool little café nearby that you'll love!"

Kartik nods, smiling back, and they head out together. Walking side by side, they make their way through the busy streets, their conversation light and easy.

Kartik (curious):
"So, how did you find this place?"

Arushi (laughing):
"I have a knack for sniffing out hidden gems. Trust me, it's worth it!"

Kartik watches her as she talks, marveling at her energy. He feels himself relaxing more with each step. By the time they arrive at the café, it feels like they've known each other forever.

❧❧❧

(Café – Afternoon)
They take a seat by the window, the sun filtering through the glass and casting a warm glow over the table. The café is cozy, with soft music playing in the background.

Arushi (leaning forward):
"So, tell me—what do you really think about this job? You've been here longer than I have. What's it really like?"

Kartik pauses, thinking for a moment before responding.

Kartik:
"It's... okay. I mean, the work is fine, and the people are nice. But sometimes, I feel like I'm just going through the motions, you know?"

Arushi (nodding):
"Yeah, I get that. It's easy to feel stuck. But I think you're doing more than just 'going through the motions.' You've got a sharp mind, Kartik. I've seen the way you handle things."

Kartik is taken aback by her directness, but he appreciates it. He feels like she sees something in him that he's been ignoring for a long time.

Kartik (softly):
"Thanks. I don't really hear that often."

Arushi smiles, her eyes warm.

Arushi:

"You should. You're more than just the 'tech guy.' You've got potential, Kartik. Don't let anyone—including yourself—tell you otherwise."

Kartik is silent for a moment, digesting her words. There's a sincerity in her tone that touches him deeply. He looks up at her, feeling a connection growing stronger with each passing second.

Kartik:

"I think... I've just been waiting. For something to change. But maybe you're right. Maybe I need to make that change myself."

Arushi (nodding firmly):

"Exactly! You're capable of so much more. You just have to take the first step."

Their food arrives, and they dig in, but the conversation doesn't falter. They talk about everything—work, life, dreams, fears. Kartik finds himself opening up to Arushi in ways he never thought possible.

Kartik (playfully):

"Okay, enough about me. What about you? What's your big dream?"

Arushi takes a sip of her drink, a thoughtful look crossing her face.

Arushi:

"Honestly? I want to start my own business one day. Something creative. I've always loved the idea of building something from the ground up."

Kartik raises an eyebrow, impressed.

Kartik:

"That's ambitious. What kind of business?"

Arushi (smiling):

"Not sure yet. Maybe a marketing consultancy, or something in design. I just want it to be something that brings people together, something that helps them grow."

Kartik watches her as she speaks, feeling inspired by her passion. There's something magnetic about the way she dreams—so vivid, so fearless.

Kartik:

"I think you'll do it. You have the drive."

Arushi (grinning):

"Thanks! I hope so. And you—what about you? What's your dream?"

Kartik hesitates, unsure of how to answer. He's spent so much time burying his own dreams, focusing on the mundane. But now, sitting across from Arushi, he feels a flicker of something he hasn't felt in a long time—hope.

Kartik:

"I guess... I'd love to build something too. Maybe not a business, but... something meaningful. Something that helps people. I'm just not sure how."

Arushi (nodding thoughtfully):

"You'll figure it out. You've got a good heart, Kartik. That's a solid foundation."

Kartik smiles, feeling a warmth spread through him. It's strange how easy it is to talk to her, how natural it feels. As they finish their lunch, Kartik realizes he's been smiling more in the last hour than he has in weeks.

(Back at the Office – Afternoon)

They return to the office together, their laughter trailing behind them. As they walk through the doors, Kartik feels a shift in the air. Things feel different—lighter.

Arushi turns to him before heading back to her desk, her eyes sparkling.

Arushi:

"That was fun. We should do it again sometime."

Kartik nods, his heart racing slightly.

Kartik:

"Yeah, definitely."

As Arushi walks away, Kartik watches her for a moment, feeling a surge of emotion he can't quite name. He sits down at his desk, but his thoughts are far from work. He can't stop thinking about Arushi—her laughter, her words, the way she seemed to understand him in a way no one else had before.

For the rest of the day, he works with renewed energy, his mind buzzing with ideas—both for work and for his life beyond the office. It's as if a door has opened, and Kartik is finally ready to step through it.

(Later – Kartik's Apartment)

That evening, Kartik sits on his couch, his laptop resting on his legs. He opens a new document, his fingers hovering over the keys. He's not sure what he's going to write, but he feels an urge to start something.

He begins typing, letting the words flow freely.

Kartik (writing):

"Sometimes, life feels like a series of small moments. Tiny, insignificant events that, when strung together, create something bigger. Today, I realized that maybe those moments aren't so small after all."

He pauses, his mind racing with thoughts of Arushi—her encouragement, her belief in him. It's strange how much her words have affected him. How much they've made him think.

Kartik (writing):

"Maybe it's time to stop waiting for something to change. Maybe it's time to make the change myself."

As he continues to write, Kartik feels a sense of clarity settling over him. He's not sure where this new path will lead, but for the first time in a long while, he's excited to find out.

CHAPTER FOUR

Unspoken Moments

(The Office – A Few Days Later)

Kartik sits at his desk, his focus shifting between work and his thoughts about Arushi. Since their lunch together, they've had several more casual meetings over coffee and lunch breaks. The more he gets to know her, the stronger his admiration grows.

Just as he's about to dive into his next task, Arushi appears at his desk, her usual bright energy lighting up the room.

Arushi (smiling):

"Hey, Kartik! We're having a small gathering at my place this weekend. Some friends, good food, maybe a few drinks. You should come!"

Kartik blinks, surprised by the invitation. He's never been one for social gatherings, especially outside of work, but the idea of spending more time with Arushi feels... different. He hesitates for a second, then nods.

Kartik:

"Yeah, sure. I'll be there."

Arushi (beaming):

"Great! You'll have fun, I promise."

She gives him a playful wink before heading back to her desk, leaving Kartik feeling both excited and nervous. This would be the first time he'd be around her outside of work, in a more personal setting.

(Saturday – Arushi's Apartment)

Kartik stands outside Arushi's apartment, holding a small bouquet of flowers as a polite gesture. He can hear laughter and music coming from inside, and his heart pounds as he raises his hand to knock on the door.

The door swings open before he gets the chance, and Arushi greets him with her signature smile.

Arushi (laughing):
"Hey! You made it. Come on in!"

Kartik steps inside, taking in the cozy atmosphere. Her apartment is warm and welcoming, decorated with personal touches that reflect her personality—colorful paintings on the walls, books stacked neatly on a shelf, and soft lighting creating a relaxed vibe.

There are a few other people in the living room, chatting and laughing. Arushi introduces him to her friends, who all seem friendly and easygoing. Kartik feels slightly out of place but tries his best to relax.

Arushi's Friend, Meera (teasing):
"So you're the famous Kartik we've heard so much about!"

Kartik glances at Arushi, who blushes slightly and shakes her head, laughing.

Arushi:
"Don't listen to her, Kartik. She loves to exaggerate."

Kartik smiles nervously but feels a little more at ease as the group welcomes him into their conversation. Soon, he's sitting on the couch, sipping a drink and listening to the lively banter between Arushi and her friends.

(Later – On the Balcony)

As the evening progresses, Kartik finds himself gravitating toward the balcony, needing a moment to collect his thoughts. The cool night air is a welcome relief from the warmth inside. He leans against the railing, staring out at the city skyline, lost in thought.

After a few minutes, the door behind him slides open, and Arushi steps outside, joining him. She stands next to him, her arms resting on the railing, and they both gaze out at the view in comfortable silence.

Arushi (softly):

"You doing okay?"

Kartik nods, his voice quiet.

Kartik:

"Yeah, just needed some air. It's nice out here."

Arushi:

"Yeah, it is. I come out here a lot when I need to think."

They fall into silence again, but it's not awkward. There's a certain ease between them that Kartik can't quite explain. After a while, Arushi breaks the quiet, her voice soft and thoughtful.

Arushi:

"You know, I've always been surrounded by people. I've got friends, family... But sometimes, I still feel kind of alone."

Kartik glances at her, surprised by the vulnerability in her tone. She rarely lets down her guard like this, and it makes him feel closer to her.

Kartik (quietly):

"I get that. I feel like that a lot, too."

Arushi turns to face him, her eyes searching his for a moment. There's something in her gaze—something unspoken but deeply felt. Kartik holds her gaze, feeling a connection that goes beyond words.

Arushi (softly):

"You're not alone, Kartik. Not anymore."

Kartik's heart skips a beat at her words, and for a brief moment, he wonders if she feels the same way he does. But before he can dwell on it, Arushi smiles and changes the subject.

Arushi:

"Come on, let's head back inside before Neha starts making wild assumptions about us out here."

Kartik chuckles, grateful for the lighthearted shift in the conversation. They return to the party, but the weight of that moment on the balcony stays with him, lingering in the back of his mind.

(Later – Kartik's Apartment)

Kartik returns home that night feeling both exhilarated and confused. The time he spent with Arushi and her friends was fun, but it was the quiet moment on the balcony that stayed with him.

He sits on his bed, replaying the conversation in his head. There was something about the way Arushi looked at him, the way she spoke... Could it be that she feels the same way? Or is he reading too much into it?

With a sigh, he opens his journal and begins to write.

Kartik (writing):

"Tonight, something shifted. I don't know what it means yet, but I feel like I'm standing on the edge of something... something that could change everything."

He closes his journal and lies back on his bed, staring at the ceiling. His mind is a whirlwind of thoughts and emotions, but one thing is clear: his feelings for Arushi are growing stronger every day.

(The Office – Monday Morning)

The next week, things between Kartik and Arushi continue as usual—at least on the surface. They still grab coffee together, exchange banter, and work on projects side by side. But there's an unspoken tension between them, a subtle shift that neither of them acknowledges outright.

One afternoon, they're working late together on a project. The office is quiet, with most of the staff having already left for the day. Kartik is typing away on his laptop when he feels Arushi's eyes on him.

Arushi (softly):

"Kartik, can I ask you something?"

Kartik looks up, meeting her gaze. There's a seriousness in her expression that makes his heart race.

Kartik (nodding):

"Yeah, of course. What's on your mind?"

Arushi (hesitating):

"Do you ever... do you ever feel like we're more than just colleagues? I mean, I know we're friends, but... sometimes I wonder if there's something else."

Kartik's heart skips a beat, his mind racing as he tries to process her words. He feels a rush of emotions—hope, fear, confusion—all at once.

Kartik (carefully):

"I've... thought about that, yeah."

Arushi looks relieved, but there's still a nervous energy in the air. She bites her lip, clearly unsure of what to say next.

Arushi:

"I don't want to complicate things, but I also don't want to pretend like I don't feel something. I don't know what it is, but it's there."

Kartik feels the weight of her words, and he knows that this is a pivotal moment. He takes a deep breath, his voice steady but soft.

Kartik:

"I feel it too, Arushi. I don't know what it means yet, but... I'm not afraid to find out."

They sit in silence for a moment, the air thick with the possibility of something new, something deeper. Neither of them knows what comes next, but they both feel the same thing: whatever happens, it will change everything.

CHAPTER FIVE

A Line Crossed

(The Office – The Next Few Days)

Kartik and Arushi's conversation about their feelings lingers between them. Neither of them has addressed it directly since that night, but the tension in the air is undeniable. Every glance, every touch, every shared moment feels charged with something more. However, both remain cautious, unsure of how to navigate these new emotions while balancing their work.

One morning, Arushi is at her desk, deep in thought, when Meera walks over, plopping down in the chair next to her.

Meera (playfully):

"Girl, what's going on with you? You've been all quiet lately. It's so unlike you."

Arushi blinks, trying to snap out of her thoughts.

Arushi (smiling faintly):

"Just work, Meera. You know how it is."

Meera raises an eyebrow, unconvinced.

Meera:

"Is that it? Or is it something to do with a certain Kartik?"

Arushi's heart skips a beat, but she quickly masks her reaction with a laugh.

Arushi:

"What? No, it's not like that."

Meera (teasing):

"Mmm-hmm, sure. You're not fooling me, Arushi. I see the way you two look at each other."

Arushi bites her lip, unsure how much to share. Meera has always been her confidante, but this situation feels delicate—too new, too undefined. She decides to downplay it, not ready to let anyone in on the complexities of her feelings just yet.

Arushi:

"It's nothing, Meera. We're just friends."

Meera rolls her eyes but drops the subject, for now.

(Kartik's Apartment – That Evening)

Kartik sits on his couch, scrolling through his phone, but his mind keeps drifting back to Arushi. He wonders if she's thinking about their conversation as much as he is. Part of him wants to bring it up again, to talk about where they stand, but another part of him is afraid of rushing things.

Suddenly, his phone buzzes. It's a message from Arushi.

Arushi (texting):

"Hey, wanna grab dinner? There's this new place I've been wanting to try."

Kartik smiles, his heart racing slightly as he types out a response.

Kartik (texting):

"Sure, I'm in. What time?"

Arushi (texting):

"8 PM. See you there!"

Kartik tosses his phone aside and heads to his room to get ready, excitement bubbling under the surface. He's nervous, but also eager to spend more time with her, especially outside of the office.

(The Restaurant – Later That Night)

Kartik arrives at the trendy new restaurant Arushi mentioned. The atmosphere is vibrant, with soft lighting, upbeat music, and the buzz of conversation. He spots Arushi at a table near the window, her face illuminated by the dim glow of the candles. She looks up as he approaches, flashing him a warm smile.

Arushi:
"Hey! You made it."

Kartik slides into the seat across from her, feeling an odd mix of comfort and nervousness. They've had dinner together countless times, but tonight feels different.

Kartik:
"Wouldn't miss it."

They order their food, and the conversation flows easily—talk of work, mutual friends, random stories from their day. But there's an underlying tension that neither of them addresses. It's as if they're both waiting for the right moment to bring up the elephant in the room.

Finally, after a brief lull in the conversation, Arushi breaks the silence.

Arushi (softly):
"Kartik, about what we talked about the other night... I've been thinking a lot about it."

Kartik sets his drink down, his full attention on her. His heart pounds, knowing that this is the moment of truth.

Kartik (quietly):
"Me too."

Arushi hesitates for a moment, gathering her thoughts before speaking.

Arushi:
"I don't want to complicate things, especially at work. But at the same time... I don't want to ignore what's happening between us."

Kartik nods, understanding the delicate balance they need to maintain. He feels the same—torn between his growing feelings for her and the fear of crossing lines that could change everything.

Kartik (gently):
"I feel the same way. But we don't have to rush into anything. We can take it slow, figure things out as we go."

Arushi smiles, relief washing over her face.

Arushi:
"Yeah. I think that's the right way to go."

They fall into a comfortable silence, the weight of their conversation lifted slightly. There's still uncertainty, but for the first time in days, Kartik feels like they're on the same page.

(The Walk Home – After Dinner)

After finishing their meal, they decide to walk back home instead of taking a cab. The night air is cool, and the streets are quieter now, giving them a sense of intimacy that wasn't there earlier.

As they walk side by side, their arms occasionally brushing, Kartik feels a sense of calm he hasn't felt in a long time. He steals a glance at Arushi, who looks deep in thought but content.

Suddenly, she stops walking and turns to face him.

Arushi (smiling):

"I'm really glad we're doing this, Kartik."

Kartik smiles back, his heart swelling with warmth.

Kartik:

"Me too."

They stand there for a moment, just looking at each other. There's something so simple, yet so significant, about this moment. Neither of them says anything more, but in the silence, there's an unspoken understanding.

Arushi takes a step closer, her fingers lightly brushing his hand. Kartik's breath catches in his throat, and for a brief second, he thinks she's going to kiss him. But she pulls back, her smile soft but playful.

Arushi (teasing):

"Goodnight, Kartik."

Kartik chuckles, feeling both relieved and disappointed.

Kartik:

"Goodnight, Arushi."

They part ways, each of them walking home with a sense of anticipation for what the future holds.

CHAPTER SIX

The Turning Point

The weekend arrived, and Kartik had invited Arushi to a local art exhibition he thought she would enjoy. He felt nervous but excited, hoping this outing would provide a chance to deepen their connection. As he stood in front of the mirror, adjusting his shirt, he could feel the butterflies fluttering in his stomach.

Kartik: (Talking to himself) "Just be yourself. She's going to love it. You got this."

As he stepped out of his house, he recalled the conversation he had with Aniket, who had encouraged him to express his feelings. The thought pushed him to keep his resolve strong.

At the gallery, Arushi arrived in a flowing sundress, her hair cascading in soft waves, looking effortlessly beautiful. When Kartik spotted her, his breath caught in his throat. She seemed to illuminate the room with her smile, and he felt an overwhelming urge to protect that light.

Kartik: (Stammering) "H-hi, Arushi! You look amazing!"

Arushi: (Blushing) "Thank you! You look great too. I'm excited to see the artwork!"

They wandered through the exhibition, discussing each piece. Arushi's insights were deep and thoughtful, and Kartik found himself hanging on her every word.

Arushi: "I love how this piece uses colors to convey emotions. It's like the artist is trying to tell a story without words."

Kartik: (Nodding) "Yeah, I see what you mean. Art really has a way of expressing what we often can't."

They paused in front of a striking painting—a vibrant landscape with dark undertones. Arushi's gaze was focused, her brow slightly furrowed in thought.

Kartik: (Curious) "What do you think it represents?"

Arushi: "I think it shows the struggle between light and darkness. It reminds me that even in tough times, there's always hope."

Kartik: (Softly) "That's beautiful. You're beautiful."

The words slipped out before he could catch himself. He turned crimson, and Arushi's eyes widened in surprise.

Arushi: (Flustered) "Kartik, I... I didn't expect that."

Kartik: (Trying to recover) "I mean—what I meant was—uh, you always see the good in everything."

They stood there, the moment stretching, both of them acutely aware of the charged atmosphere. Then Meera's voice broke the tension as she approached them, her grin wide.

Meera: "Well, if it isn't the lovebirds! Enjoying the art and each other's company, I see?"

Kartik shot Meera a warning look, but Arushi laughed, easing the awkwardness.

Arushi: "We're just appreciating the art, Meera. Right, Kartik?"

Kartik: (Nervously) "Yeah, just the art."

Meera raised an eyebrow, clearly not buying it but choosing to let it go for now. She glanced at the painting they had been discussing.

Meera: "You two are too cute. Let's take a photo together!"

They posed in front of the painting, Arushi's laughter ringing out as Meera nudged Kartik closer to her.

Meera: "Smile, you two! This will be a memory!"

As the camera clicked, Kartik caught Arushi's gaze and felt his heart race again. Was this the moment to finally confess?

After the exhibition, they decided to grab coffee at a nearby café. Seated outside, the sun began to set, painting the sky in hues of orange and pink.

Arushi: (Sipping her coffee) "Today was really fun. I loved seeing the art with you."

Kartik: (Gaining courage) "I'm glad you enjoyed it. I wanted to ask... do you think we could do this more often? Just us?"

Arushi looked thoughtful for a moment, her eyes sparkling with interest.

Arushi: "I'd like that. I really would."

Kartik's heart soared. They were on the right track, but the words still hung in the air, unspoken yet palpable.

Later that night, Kartik sat in his room, replaying the day's events. He picked up his phone, his fingers hovering over the screen, contemplating a message to Aniket.

Kartik: (Texting) "Hey, just got back from the exhibition with Arushi. I think I'm falling for her."

As he hit send, he felt a sense of relief wash over him. He was ready to take a chance, even if it meant risking his heart.

CHAPTER SEVEN

The Confession

The following week, the atmosphere in the office felt charged. Kartik noticed Arushi more than ever, and each interaction seemed to bring them closer. However, the fear of confessing still lingered in the back of his mind. Meanwhile, Meera was up to her usual antics, playfully nudging Arushi toward Kartik at every opportunity.

One afternoon, while they were all gathered for lunch, Meera leaned over to Arushi.

Meera: (Whispering) "You know, I think you should tell him how you feel. He's crazy about you!"

Arushi: (Fidgeting) "But what if he doesn't feel the same? I can't handle that kind of rejection."

Before Meera could respond, Kartik entered the lunchroom, his presence commanding attention. He took a seat next to Arushi, his heart racing as he caught her eye.

Kartik: "Hey, guys! Hope I'm not interrupting anything."

Meera: (Winking at Arushi) "Not at all. Just girl talk."

Kartik raised an eyebrow, clearly curious but choosing to let it slide.

Kartik: "So, any plans for the weekend?"

The conversation flowed, but Kartik found it increasingly difficult to focus. He felt an intense desire to speak his truth, but the words tangled in his throat.

As lunch ended, Arushi stood to leave, and Kartik felt a surge of determination.

Kartik: (Calling out) "Arushi, can we talk for a minute?"

She turned, surprise dancing in her eyes but a smile on her lips.

Arushi: "Sure, what's up?"

They stepped into a quieter corner of the office, and Kartik's heart raced as he gathered his thoughts. He could feel the weight of the moment pressing down on him.

Kartik: (Nervously) "I've been thinking a lot about us... about what we have. I really enjoy spending time with you."

Arushi: (Her heart racing) "Me too, Kartik. I really do."

Kartik took a deep breath, steeling himself.

Kartik: "I think I've started to develop feelings for you. More than just friends. I just needed you to know that."

Arushi's breath caught in her throat. She hadn't expected him to say it so directly, but her heart fluttered with hope.

Arushi: (Softly) "You don't know how much I wanted to hear that. I've felt the same way, but I was so scared."

Kartik's eyes widened, and for a moment, time seemed to freeze around them.

Kartik: "Really? You mean it?"

Arushi: (Nodding) "Yes! I was just waiting for the right moment, and I guess you just made it happen."

As they stood there, a wave of relief washed over Kartik. They had taken the leap together, and it felt like the beginning of something beautiful.

CHAPTER EIGHT

The First Date

The weight of their mutual confession hung sweetly in the air, and everything between Kartik and Arushi felt different now. Even the most casual interactions were laced with a new kind of excitement, and both of them knew that this was just the beginning of something deeper. The very next day, Kartik had mustered up the courage to ask Arushi out on a proper date.

Kartik: (Smiling nervously) "So... would you like to go out for dinner with me this Saturday? Just the two of us?"

Arushi's eyes sparkled, a soft smile lighting up her face.

Arushi: "I'd love that."

And just like that, their first real date was set.

Saturday evening arrived, and Kartik was pacing around his room, trying to calm his nerves. He looked at himself in the mirror, straightening his shirt for the third time.

Aniket: (On the phone) "Dude, calm down! It's just dinner. You've already confessed, so the hard part is over."

Kartik chuckled, but he couldn't shake the excitement buzzing under his skin.

Kartik: "I know, I know... but it feels huge. This is our first date, man!"

Aniket: "Relax, you're going to be fine. Just be yourself and enjoy it."

Kartik took a deep breath, thanking Aniket for his pep talk, and then headed out to pick up Arushi.

When Kartik arrived at Arushi's place, he was struck silent by how stunning she looked. She wore a simple yet elegant dress, her hair flowing in soft waves, and a shy smile on her lips when she noticed the way he was staring.

Kartik: (Awkwardly) "You... look amazing."

Arushi: (Blushing) "Thank you, Kartik. You look great too."

They shared a shy smile before Kartik opened the car door for her, a small, nervous gesture that Arushi found endearing.

They arrived at a cozy restaurant, one of Kartik's favorites. It was a quiet place, perfect for intimate conversations, with warm lighting and a welcoming atmosphere. As they sat down, the initial nerves began to settle, and soon they were talking like they always did—effortlessly.

Arushi: "I can't believe this is our first date. It feels like we've known each other forever."

Kartik: (Smiling) "Yeah, it does. But it also feels different now, in a good way."

As they ordered their food, the conversation flowed smoothly, touching on everything from their favorite movies to their childhood memories. The more they talked, the more Kartik realized how deep his feelings for her had become. He wasn't just attracted to her—he admired her, respected her, and was captivated by the way she saw the world.

At one point, the conversation turned to their confession from the other day. Kartik hesitated, but decided to ask what had been on his mind.

Kartik: "So... when did you realize you felt the same way?"

Arushi looked thoughtful for a moment before answering.

Arushi: "I think I always liked you, Kartik, but I wasn't sure if it was just friendship. Then, as we spent more time together, I realized how much I cared about you... more than I ever did for anyone else. But I was afraid to say anything because I didn't want to ruin what we had."

Kartik: (Nodding) "I felt the same. I didn't want to risk losing you as a friend."

Arushi reached across the table, her hand gently covering his.

Arushi: "I'm glad you took the risk."

Kartik smiled, his heart swelling with affection as their hands lingered together on the table.

The rest of the night flew by, and before they knew it, they were walking out of the restaurant. The cool evening breeze brushed against them, and Kartik found himself wanting the night to never end. As they walked to his car, he hesitated for a moment, then turned to face her.

Kartik: "I had a really great time tonight, Arushi. I don't think I've ever enjoyed a dinner this much."

Arushi: (Laughing softly) "Me too. It was perfect."

They stood there, the moment stretching between them. Kartik could feel the pull between them, the unspoken connection that had been building for so long. Slowly, he stepped closer, his hand reaching up to gently tuck a loose strand of hair behind Arushi's ear.

Kartik: (Softly) "I really like you, Arushi."

Arushi's breath caught in her throat as she gazed up at him, her heart racing.

Arushi: (Whispering) "I like you too, Kartik."

Their faces were inches apart, the air thick with anticipation. Kartik's hand cupped her cheek, and for a brief moment, time seemed to stand still. Then, gently, he leaned in and kissed her. It was soft, tentative, but full of emotion—a kiss that spoke of everything they hadn't said out loud.

When they pulled apart, both of them were smiling, their hearts pounding in unison.

Arushi: (Breathlessly) "That was... perfect."

Kartik: (Smiling) "I've wanted to do that for a while."

They stood there for a moment longer, basking in the glow of their new relationship. It was just the beginning, but it already felt like everything they had been waiting for.

As Kartik drove her home, the radio played softly in the background, but neither of them said much. They didn't need to. The silence between them was comfortable, full of unspoken promises and shared emotions.

When they arrived at Arushi's place, she turned to him, her eyes soft and warm.

Arushi: "Thanks for tonight, Kartik. It was perfect."

Kartik: (Smiling) "Anytime. I'll see you tomorrow?"

Arushi: (Nodding) "Definitely."

With one last, lingering smile, Arushi stepped out of the car and headed inside, leaving Kartik sitting there with his heart full and his mind spinning. As he drove home, he couldn't stop grinning. This was it—the start of something beautiful.

CHAPTER NINE

Navigating New Feelings

Kartik woke up with a smile plastered on his face, his mind replaying every moment of the previous night. He grabbed his phone, almost instinctively, and saw a message from Arushi.

Arushi's Text:

"Good morning! ? Last night was perfect. Can't wait to see you today. What's your plan?"

Kartik felt a rush of happiness. He quickly replied:

Kartik's Text:

"Morning! Last night was amazing. I'm free today. Want to grab coffee or hang out somewhere?"

Meanwhile, Arushi was feeling the same excitement. She stared at her phone after sending the message, her heart doing flips. The night before was magical, and the fact that she had kissed Kartik—something she had only imagined—made everything feel so surreal.

She quickly responded:

Arushi's Text:

"How about a walk in the park, then coffee? It's such a nice day out!"

Kartik smiled and immediately agreed. Within an hour, they were walking side by side, enjoying the greenery of the nearby park. The sun shone brightly, and the air was filled with the pleasant chirping of birds. The atmosphere was serene, but the nervous excitement between them was still very much alive.

Kartik: (Laughing softly) "So, what's on your mind? You've been quiet since we met."

Arushi: (Grinning) "I've just been thinking... last night was amazing, right? I can't stop thinking about it."

Kartik blushed slightly, nodding in agreement.

Kartik: "Same here. It feels like... everything's changed but also like it's always been this way."

They reached a bench, sat down, and faced each other. Kartik could see the light reflecting in Arushi's eyes, and for a moment, he just watched her, taking in how much she meant to him. There was something so comforting about her presence.

As they talked, Arushi's phone buzzed. It was a message from Meera.

Meera's Text:

"Tell me EVERYTHING! How did the date go? ?"

Arushi laughed softly, showing the message to Kartik.

Arushi: "Meera's dying to know how things went."

Kartik chuckled, shaking his head.

Kartik: "You should tell her it was a disaster. Just to mess with her."

Arushi raised an eyebrow, amused by the idea.

Arushi: "She'd probably come running over to interrogate me!"

They both laughed, the easy banter easing any lingering awkwardness. Arushi texted Meera back, letting her know the date was perfect and promising to give her all the details later.

After spending some time at the park, they headed to a nearby café. The conversation between them grew deeper as they sipped their coffee.

Kartik: "So, do you ever think about what's next for us?"

The question hung in the air for a moment, and Arushi set her cup down, thinking carefully before she answered.

Arushi: "Honestly, I haven't thought too far ahead. I've just been enjoying the moment, you know? But now that we've started this... I guess we'll just see where it goes, right?"

Kartik nodded, appreciating her honesty. He hadn't thought too much about the future either, but now that they had confessed their feelings, it was natural to wonder what would come next.

Kartik: "Yeah... I feel the same. I just want to take it one day at a time with you."

They shared a smile, the weight of expectations lifted off their shoulders. It was clear that neither of them wanted to rush things, and that was comforting in its own way.

❧❧❧

The rest of the day was spent exploring the city, stopping at little shops and enjoying each other's company. By the time the sun began to set, they found themselves back at the park, sitting on the same bench they had earlier.

There was a peaceful silence between them, both content just to be near each other.

Arushi: (Leaning on his shoulder) "This feels... nice."

Kartik: (Gently) "Yeah, it does."

For a moment, neither of them spoke. The breeze rustled the leaves above them, and the sun dipped lower in the sky, casting a warm glow over everything.

Arushi: (Softly) "I think I've always been waiting for someone like you, Kartik. Someone who sees me for who I am, not just for how I look."

Kartik's heart swelled at her words. He placed his arm around her, pulling her a little closer.

Kartik: "And I've been waiting for someone like you. You make me feel... like I'm enough. Like I don't have to be more than who I already am."

Arushi smiled, and they sat there for a long time, watching the sunset, basking in the quiet understanding that their relationship, though new, was built on something strong.

CHAPTER TEN

Friends and Fears

While everything seemed perfect between Kartik and Arushi, Kartik couldn't help but feel a small sense of worry gnawing at him. What if things changed? What if they lost the magic they'd found? These thoughts kept him awake at night, though he never let on when he was with Arushi.

One day, as they were sitting together at a café, Kartik's phone buzzed. It was Aniket.

Aniket's Text:
"How's it going with Arushi, man? We need to catch up!"

Kartik smiled, realizing that it had been a while since he'd spoken to his best friend. He replied quickly.

Kartik's Text:
"It's going great. Let's meet up soon!"

Later that evening, Kartik met up with Aniket at their favorite spot. Aniket grinned as soon as Kartik sat down.

Aniket: "So, tell me everything! How's it going with you and Arushi?"

Kartik laughed, shaking his head.

Kartik: "It's good. Really good, actually. But... I don't know. I've been overthinking things."

Aniket raised an eyebrow, leaning forward.

Aniket: "Overthinking? What's there to overthink?"

Kartik sighed, rubbing the back of his neck.

Kartik: "I just... I don't want to mess this up. What if things change between us? What if we don't work out in the long run?"

Aniket gave him a reassuring smile.

Aniket: "Listen, man. You can't think like that. You two are good together. Just enjoy it. You don't have to have all the answers right now."

Kartik nodded, appreciating his friend's words. Aniket was right—he was overthinking things. He needed to let go of the fear and just focus on what he had with Arushi.

That night, as Kartik lay in bed, he replayed the conversation with Aniket in his mind. He realized that worrying about the future was only robbing him of the happiness he had right now. And right now, Arushi made him happier than he had ever been.

CHAPTER ELEVEN

Secrets Between Hearts

The next few days passed by in a blur of coffee dates, late-night conversations, and stolen glances. Kartik and Arushi were undeniably drawn to each other. But as close as they were getting, there was something unspoken between them—something Kartik couldn't quite shake off. It wasn't anything Arushi had said or done. Rather, it was what she hadn't said.

Kartik noticed Arushi would sometimes get distant, her smile fading into a pensive expression. She would change the subject whenever their conversations took a serious turn, especially when it came to her past. He didn't want to push her, but curiosity gnawed at him. Was she hiding something? Or was she just cautious about opening up completely?

One afternoon, Kartik and Arushi decided to visit a nearby art gallery that had just opened. Arushi had been excited about it for days, and Kartik was eager to spend more time with her in a place that seemed so close to her heart.

As they walked through the gallery, admiring the vibrant paintings and abstract sculptures, Kartik noticed how deeply Arushi seemed connected to the art around her. Her eyes would light up at certain pieces, and she'd spend long moments staring at others, lost in thought.

Kartik: (Smiling) "You're really into this, huh? I've never seen you so quiet."

Arushi chuckled softly, shaking her head.

Arushi: "Yeah, I guess I am. Art has always been a kind of... escape for me. It lets you feel things that you can't always put into words."

Kartik nodded, glancing at the painting she was staring at—a portrait of a woman standing on the edge of a cliff, looking out over the ocean, her expression unreadable.

Kartik: (Gently) "What does it make you feel?"

Arushi didn't answer immediately. Her gaze remained fixed on the painting, her brow furrowing slightly as if she was wrestling with her thoughts.

Arushi: "It makes me feel... like that woman's waiting for something. Or maybe someone. Like she's got a lot of emotions bottled up inside, but she's afraid to let them out."

Kartik studied Arushi's face as she spoke, sensing there was more to her words than she was letting on. He wanted to ask her if she felt like that sometimes—if there were things she wasn't telling him. But he didn't. Not yet.

❧❧❧

After the gallery visit, they headed to a nearby café for a late lunch. The conversation was light at first, but Kartik couldn't shake off the feeling that there was something Arushi wasn't telling him.

Kartik: (After a long pause) "Arushi... can I ask you something?"

Arushi looked up from her coffee, sensing the shift in his tone.

Arushi: "Sure, Kartik. What's up?"

Kartik hesitated for a moment, choosing his words carefully.

Kartik: "You don't have to answer if you're not ready, but... I've noticed that sometimes you get really quiet. Like there's something on your mind that you're not telling me. I don't want to pry, but I also want to understand you better."

Arushi blinked, her expression guarded for a moment before she sighed softly.

Arushi: "It's not that I don't trust you, Kartik. I do. It's just... there are some things about my past that I'm not sure how to talk about yet."

Kartik nodded slowly, not wanting to push her further.

Kartik: "Whenever you're ready, I'll be here to listen."

Arushi smiled at him, though it didn't quite reach her eyes. Kartik could see that whatever she was holding back, it wasn't easy for her to talk about. But he knew that pushing her wouldn't help. He had to be patient.

Later that evening, after parting ways with Arushi, Kartik found himself thinking about their conversation. He wanted to be there for her, to help her through whatever she was dealing with, but he also knew that it wasn't something he could force. People opened up in their own time.

As he was scrolling through his phone absentmindedly, a message from Meera popped up.

Meera's Text:

"So, how are things going with Arushi? Still going strong?"

Kartik smiled, shaking his head. Meera always had a way of getting straight to the point. He replied:

Kartik's Text:

"Yeah, things are good. Really good. But I think she's holding back something from her past. I don't know what, and I don't want to push her, but it's hard not to wonder."

Meera's response came almost immediately.

Meera's Text:

"She's been through some tough stuff, Kartik. I don't know all the details, but I do know that when Arushi finally opens up, it's because she really trusts you. Give her time."

Kartik appreciated Meera's words. He knew she and Arushi were close, and if anyone could understand what was going on, it was Meera. He decided to take her advice to heart.

Days turned into weeks, and though things were still wonderful between Kartik and Arushi, there was always that undercurrent of mystery hanging between them. Kartik tried to focus on the positive, enjoying every moment he spent with her, but his mind couldn't help but wander back to the things she wasn't saying.

One evening, they were out for a casual dinner when Kartik noticed a subtle shift in Arushi's demeanor. She seemed tense, distracted even, as if her mind was somewhere else entirely.

Kartik: (Gently) "Hey, you okay? You seem a little... off tonight."

Arushi blinked, snapping out of her thoughts. She offered a small smile, but it didn't quite reach her eyes.

Arushi: "Yeah, sorry. I'm just... thinking about some stuff."

Kartik didn't press her, but he gave her hand a reassuring squeeze.

Kartik: "You know I'm here for you, right? Whatever it is, you don't have to deal with it alone."

Arushi looked at him for a long moment, her eyes filled with a mix of gratitude and something else—something heavier, deeper.

Arushi: "I know. And I appreciate that, Kartik. I really do. It's just... some things are hard to talk about, you know?"

Kartik nodded, understanding that she wasn't ready yet. But he also knew that when she was, he'd be there, ready to listen.

That night, as Kartik lay in bed, staring at the ceiling, he couldn't help but wonder what Arushi was going through. He knew that everyone had their own battles, their own scars. But it was hard not to feel a little helpless when the person you cared about was hurting and you didn't know how to make it better.

He sighed, rolling over and grabbing his phone. Without thinking too much, he typed out a message to Arushi.

Kartik's Text:

"I know you're dealing with stuff, and I just want you to know that whenever you're ready, I'll be here. No pressure. Just... whenever you're ready."

He hit send, then placed his phone on the bedside table, closing his eyes and willing himself to sleep. He didn't expect a response right away, but just knowing that he had reached out made him feel a little better.

The next morning, Kartik woke up to find a message from Arushi waiting for him.

Arushi's Text:
"Thank you, Kartik. I'll talk to you soon. I promise."

Kartik smiled softly at the message, his heart warming at her words. He knew it would take time, but he was willing to wait. After all, some things were worth waiting for.

CHAPTER TWELVE

The Past Unveiled

Kartik and Arushi's relationship continued to grow, but the air between them was charged with a tension neither could ignore. Kartik remained patient, never pressing Arushi to open up before she was ready. But he knew that sooner or later, the past would have to be addressed.

One chilly afternoon, as they sat together in a cozy café, sipping on hot chocolate, Arushi finally took a deep breath and turned to Kartik, her eyes filled with uncertainty.

Arushi: (Softly) "Kartik... there's something I need to tell you."

Kartik's heart skipped a beat as Arushi spoke those words. Her voice was soft, almost hesitant, and it filled the space between them with a weight he hadn't expected. He had been waiting for this moment, but now that it was here, he wasn't sure he was ready. Still, he nodded, his eyes locked on hers, offering her the reassurance that whatever she had to say, he was there to listen.

Kartik: (Gently) "Take your time, Arushi. I'm listening."

Arushi looked down at her hands, fidgeting with the edge of her scarf. She took a deep breath, as if trying to steady herself, and when she spoke again, her voice was quiet, almost fragile.

Arushi: "Before I met you, I was in a relationship. It was... intense. We were together for a long time, and I thought he was the one. But things started to change. He became controlling, manipulative. I didn't see it at first because I was so wrapped up in him. But slowly, he began to isolate me from my friends, my family. He made me feel like I wasn't enough, like I had to prove my worth to him over and over again."

Kartik's chest tightened as he listened to her words, the pain in her voice cutting through him. He could see how difficult it was for her to relive these memories, and he reached across the table, taking her hand in his.

Kartik: (Softly) "I'm so sorry you went through that."

Arushi nodded, her eyes still downcast. She squeezed his hand, as if drawing strength from his touch.

Arushi: "It wasn't easy. I kept thinking if I just loved him more, or tried harder, he would change. But it never got better. It got worse. He started to get... aggressive. Not physically, but emotionally. He knew how to hurt me with words. How to make me feel small. I was trapped in that cycle for so long that I didn't even recognize myself anymore."

Kartik's mind reeled. He couldn't imagine someone treating Arushi like that, breaking her down piece by piece. She was so strong, so independent. But as she shared her story, he realized that strength didn't mean she hadn't been hurt. It just meant she had found a way to survive.

Kartik: (With empathy) "How did you get out?"

Arushi finally lifted her gaze to meet his. Her eyes were glassy, but there was a spark of resilience in them.

Arushi: "It took a lot. I had to hit rock bottom first. I was isolated, and I had no one left. That's when Meera came back into my life. She noticed something was wrong and wouldn't let me push her away again. She helped me see what I couldn't—what I didn't want to admit to myself. With her support, I found the courage to leave him. It wasn't easy. He didn't take it well. But I knew I had to save myself."

Kartik felt a wave of gratitude toward Meera. She had been there for Arushi when she needed someone most, and now, Arushi was here, stronger, rebuilding her life.

Kartik: "I'm glad you had Meera. And I'm even more glad that you had the strength to walk away."

Arushi smiled weakly, but it was a smile of relief, as if a heavy burden had been lifted by sharing her story.

Arushi: "That's why I've been so guarded, Kartik. It's not that I don't care about you. It's just... I've been hurt before. I don't want to rush into something and end up in the same place again."

Kartik nodded, his heart aching for her, but also filled with admiration for her courage. He understood now why she had been so careful, so hesitant to open up completely. And he knew that if he wanted to be with her, he would have to be patient, to give her the space and time she needed.

Kartik: (Gently) "I get it, Arushi. And I don't want to rush you into anything. We can take this slow, whatever pace feels right for you. I just want you to know that I'm here, and I'm not going anywhere."

Arushi's eyes softened, and for the first time in what felt like weeks, Kartik saw a glimmer of the Arushi he had first fallen for—the one who smiled easily, who was confident and unafraid. She leaned across the table, pressing her hand against his cheek.

Arushi: "Thank you, Kartik. You have no idea how much that means to me."

Over the next few days, something shifted between Kartik and Arushi. The air was lighter, the tension that had lingered between them now dissipating. Arushi was more open, more present, and Kartik noticed how much more comfortable she seemed in his presence. But there were still moments when she would retreat into herself, moments when the shadow of her past would cast a pall over her, and Kartik would patiently wait for her to come back.

One evening, as they walked through the park, the golden hues of the sunset casting long shadows on the ground, Kartik felt a strange sense of peace. They had talked about everything and nothing all at once, and for the first time in a long while, there were no lingering doubts, no unspoken fears. Just them.

Kartik glanced at Arushi, who was watching the sky with a soft smile on her face. Her hand was resting in his, their fingers intertwined. He felt the words bubbling up inside him, words he hadn't allowed himself to fully acknowledge until now. And though he was scared of what it might mean, he couldn't hold them back any longer.

Kartik: (Softly) "Arushi... I think I'm falling in love with you."

The words hung in the air between them, delicate and fragile, as if they might shatter if he breathed too hard. He waited, his heart pounding in his chest, unsure of what she would say.

Arushi turned to him, her eyes wide with surprise. For a moment, she didn't speak, and Kartik's heart sank, wondering if he had made a mistake.

But then she smiled—a real, genuine smile—and he felt a rush of relief wash over him.

Arushi: (Whispering) "Kartik, I... I think I'm falling in love with you too."

Kartik's breath caught in his throat. He hadn't expected her to say it back—not yet, at least. But hearing those words made his heart soar. He pulled her into his arms, holding her tightly as if afraid that if he let go, this moment would slip away.

They stood there for a long time, wrapped in each other's embrace as the sun dipped below the horizon, casting the world in shades of purple and gold. For the first time in a long time, Kartik felt like everything was right in the world.

CHAPTER THIRTEEN

Unspoken Feelings

Kartik and Arushi's living room. Soft music plays in the background. The air is filled with unspoken tension as they sit together on the couch.

Kartik: (breaking the silence) "You know, it's funny. We've shared so much, yet there's still so much left unsaid."

Arushi: (nodding) "I feel it too. Sometimes I wonder if we're just scared of what those words might change."

Kartik: (looking thoughtful) "What if we say them anyway? What if we just... put everything on the table?"

Arushi: (pausing) "That sounds risky. But maybe it's time for us to be honest with each other."

Kartik: (leaning closer) "I think we owe it to ourselves. We've already crossed so many lines; why not this one?"

Arushi: (smiling softly) "Okay. I'll start. I... I've been feeling something for a while now, something more than just friendship."

Kartik: (heart racing) "Really? I thought I was the only one. I've been afraid to say it because... what if it ruins everything?"

Arushi: (reaching for his hand) "But what if it makes everything better? What if we're meant to be more than friends?"

Kartik: (squeezing her hand) "I want that too. I care about you, Arushi, more than I ever thought possible."

Arushi: (tearing up) "You have no idea how long I've waited to hear you say that."

Kartik: (smiling) "So, where do we go from here? What do we do with these feelings?"

Arushi: "Let's take it slow. We don't have to rush into anything. Just being honest is a huge step."

Kartik: (nodding) "Agreed. I'm okay with taking things at our own pace."

As they talk, the atmosphere shifts. They start laughing and sharing stories, the tension transforming into warmth and connection.

Kartik: "You know, I've always admired how you see the world. You make everything seem brighter."

Arushi: "And you have this incredible ability to understand people, to make them feel valued. It's rare."

Kartik: "Maybe that's what makes us work so well together. We complement each other."

Arushi: (grinning) "Exactly. I guess we're just better together."

Kartik: (playfully) "Better together, huh? Sounds like a good tagline for a couple."

Arushi: (laughing) "Definitely! Let's make it our motto."

The two share a light-hearted moment, their laughter filling the room, a sign of their newfound connection.

As the night wears on, they decide to take a walk outside. The stars twinkle above them, and the cool breeze carries the scent of blooming flowers.

Kartik: "Look at the stars, Arushi. It's like they're cheering for us."

Arushi: "I know! It's perfect. I feel like anything is possible right now."

Kartik: "And it all started with us being brave enough to speak our truths."

Arushi: "Here's to more honesty and deeper connections."

Kartik: (smiling) "And to whatever comes next."

CHAPTER FOURTEEN

Crossing New Thresholds

The following week, the sun shone brightly as Kartik and Arushi met at their favorite café. The atmosphere was buzzing with energy, and the aroma of freshly brewed coffee filled the air.

Arushi: (looking around) "I love this place. It always feels like the perfect escape."

Kartik: (smiling) "Yeah, it has its charm. Just like you."

Arushi: (playfully rolling her eyes) "Stop it! You're making me blush."

Kartik: "What? It's true! You brighten up the room the moment you walk in."

Arushi: (laughing) "Okay, you win. Let's order something before I get too flattered."

As they placed their orders, Arushi noticed a couple sitting nearby, clearly in love. She watched them share a dessert and laughed, feeling a pang of longing.

Arushi: (turning to Kartik) "Do you ever think about how amazing it would be to have a love like that? Just... effortless and full of joy?"

Kartik: (nodding) "I do. But I think every relationship has its struggles, too. It's about how you face them together."

Arushi: "You're right. I guess every love story has its ups and downs. What matters is the connection."

Their drinks arrived, and they both took a moment to enjoy the warmth of their cups.

Kartik: (leaning forward) "Speaking of connections, how do you feel about us? About what we talked about the other night?"

Arushi: (pausing) "I'm excited, but also a bit nervous. It's a big step."

Kartik: (earnestly) "I know, but I'm willing to take that step if you are. I want to explore where this goes."

Arushi: (smiling) "I want that too, Kartik. But can we promise to be open and honest with each other? No matter what happens?"

Kartik: "Absolutely. That's the foundation of any relationship, right?"

Arushi: "Right. Let's build something beautiful together."

After their heartfelt conversation, they decided to take a stroll in the nearby park. The vibrant colors of spring surrounded them, and the laughter of children playing filled the air.

Kartik: (pointing at a playground) "Look at those kids! They're having the time of their lives."

Arushi: (giggling) "I remember when we used to play like that. Everything seemed so simple back then."

Kartik: "Yeah, carefree. It's nice to let go of adult worries for a while."

As they continued walking, they came across a small lake with ducks swimming lazily.

Arushi: "This place is so peaceful. It's like a little slice of paradise."

Kartik: (smiling) "Just like you."

Arushi: (teasing) "You're really on a roll today, aren't you?"

Kartik: "Just being honest! You deserve to hear it."

Suddenly, Arushi's phone buzzed. She checked it and frowned.

Arushi: "It's from work. I need to take this." (she steps aside to take the call)

Kartik watched her, his heart sinking slightly. He hoped this wouldn't disrupt their day. After a few minutes, she returned, looking slightly distressed.

Arushi: "I'm sorry about that. Just some issues at the office. I'll handle it later."

Kartik: "Everything okay?"

Arushi: (sighing) "Yeah, it will be. Just a bit overwhelming."

Kartik: (reassuringly) "You can always talk to me about it, you know?"

Arushi: (nodding) "I appreciate that. It helps to have someone who cares."

As they walked further, the conversation shifted to lighter topics. They joked about their childhood dreams and shared funny stories from school. Kartik felt a weight lift off his shoulders, grateful for the easy camaraderie they had.

Kartik: "If you could have any superpower, what would it be?"

Arushi: (thinking) "Hmm, maybe the ability to teleport. Just imagine the adventures we could have!"

Kartik: (laughing) "Teleporting would be amazing! We could travel anywhere in an instant."

Arushi: (grinning) "Right? But we'd have to figure out how to teleport to our meetings too!"

They both burst into laughter, their worries momentarily forgotten. As they continued their stroll, Arushi felt grateful for this day, for Kartik's presence, and for the connection they were building.

Kartik: "You know, I feel like I've known you forever."

Arushi: (smiling) "Same here. It's like we've always been meant to find each other."

Kartik: (looking into her eyes) "Let's promise to keep discovering each other, no matter where this journey takes us."

Arushi: (nodding) "Deal. Here's to new beginnings."

CHAPTER FIFTEEN

Unraveling Dreams

As the days turned into weeks, Kartik and Arushi grew more comfortable in their relationship. Each meeting was filled with laughter, shared stories, and moments of silent understanding. However, beneath the surface of their budding romance, both were grappling with their insecurities.

One evening, they decided to have a cozy movie night at Kartik's place. He had set up a projector in his living room, creating an intimate atmosphere. As they settled down on the couch with popcorn, Kartik noticed the tension in Arushi's eyes.

Kartik: "You okay, Arushi? You seem a bit distant."

Arushi: (sighing) "Yeah, just thinking about everything. You know how I mentioned my work stress? It's been weighing on me."

Kartik: "You can talk to me about it. I want to be there for you."

Arushi: (smiling softly) "I know, and I appreciate it. It's just... sometimes I feel like I'm juggling too many things at once."

Kartik: (nodding) "Life can get overwhelming. But remember, you don't have to handle everything alone."

Arushi: "I keep telling myself that, but it's hard to let go of control."

Kartik: (taking her hand) "Let's tackle it together. We can create a plan for your workload, and you can take breaks when you need to."

Arushi: (looking at him) "You really mean that?"

Kartik: "Of course! I'm not just here for the fun times. I want to support you through the tough moments too."

Arushi felt a warmth spread through her as she looked into his earnest eyes. She squeezed his hand, grateful for his unwavering support.

Arushi: "Thank you, Kartik. It really means a lot."

They began the movie, but Arushi's mind kept drifting. The film played on, yet she couldn't shake off the feeling that her fears were catching up to her. After the first hour, she paused the movie.

Arushi: "Can we talk?"

Kartik: (concerned) "Sure. What's on your mind?"

Arushi: "I've been thinking about us and how quickly things have progressed. I'm really happy, but part of me is scared."

Kartik: "Scared of what?"

Arushi: "What if this doesn't last? What if I end up getting hurt?"

Kartik: (sighing) "I get it. It's natural to feel that way when you're investing in someone. But I want you to know that I'm serious about this. I'm not going anywhere."

Arushi: "It's just that I've been hurt before, and I don't want to feel that pain again."

Kartik: "I promise to be honest with you and communicate openly. If something feels off, we'll address it together."

Arushi nodded, appreciating his reassurance. She took a deep breath, gathering her thoughts.

Arushi: "I want to believe that. I really do."

Kartik: "Let's make a pact. No matter what, we'll keep the lines of communication open. We'll check in with each other regularly."

Arushi: "That sounds fair. I like that idea."

Kartik: "Good. Now, let's get back to the movie. We can tackle our fears later!"

They resumed the film, and as the story unfolded, they found solace in each other's presence. After the movie, they decided to take a walk outside. The cool evening air was refreshing, and the stars twinkled overhead.

Kartik: "Look at those stars! They remind me of dreams—each one representing something we aspire to achieve."

Arushi: "That's a beautiful thought. Do you have dreams you're chasing?"

Kartik: "Definitely. I want to build a life that aligns with my values. I want to make a difference in the world, even if it's in small ways."

Arushi: "I admire that about you. You have such a kind heart."

Kartik: "And you inspire me too. Your strength and passion are contagious."

They walked in comfortable silence, allowing the beauty of the night to envelop them. Eventually, they found a bench and sat down.

Kartik: "What about you? What dreams do you hold close?"

Arushi: (pausing) "I've always wanted to make an impact in my field. I want to help people, but I also want to stay true to myself."

Kartik: "You're already doing that by being yourself. Your authenticity shines through."

Arushi: (smiling) "Thanks, Kartik. I feel like I can be my true self with you."

Kartik: "That's how it should be. No facades, just genuine connection."

They both sat quietly for a moment, watching the stars. Then, Arushi felt a sudden surge of emotions. She turned to Kartik, her heart racing.

Arushi: "Kartik, can I tell you something?"

Kartik: "Of course. What's on your mind?"

Arushi: "I think I'm starting to fall for you."

Kartik's heart skipped a beat. He turned to face her fully, his expression serious yet filled with warmth.

Kartik: "I feel the same way, Arushi. I really do."

Arushi: "It scares me, but it also excites me. I've never felt this way before."

Kartik: "Me neither. But I want to explore this feeling together, wherever it takes us."

Arushi: "I'd like that. Let's take it one day at a time."

Kartik: "Exactly. One day at a time."

As they shared a smile, the world around them faded. In that moment, under the vast sky filled with dreams, they felt a connection deeper than words could express. They both knew that their journey was just beginning, filled with possibilities, challenges, and the magic of discovering love.

CHAPTER SIXTEEN

The Tides of Change

As the days rolled into weeks, Kartik and Arushi found a rhythm in their relationship. Their bond grew stronger, yet beneath the surface, life continued to throw challenges their way. The summer break was approaching, and with it came a flurry of changes that neither of them had anticipated.

One sunny afternoon, while sitting in their favorite café, Arushi looked particularly contemplative. She stirred her coffee absentmindedly, her brow furrowed.

Kartik: "You seem lost in thought today. What's going on in that beautiful mind of yours?"

Arushi: (looking up, startled) "Oh, sorry! I was just thinking about the upcoming summer break and how things might change."

Kartik: "Change isn't always bad. What specifically are you worried about?"

Arushi took a deep breath, gathering her thoughts.

Arushi: "Well, I have an internship opportunity lined up, which is amazing, but it's in a different city. It would mean moving away for the summer."

Kartik's heart sank at the thought of Arushi being away, even temporarily.

Kartik: "Wow, that sounds like an incredible opportunity! But... how do you feel about it?"

Arushi: "I'm excited, but I'm also scared. What if it changes everything between us?"

Kartik: "Distance can be tough, but it can also strengthen a relationship. We can make it work, right?"

Arushi: "I hope so. I just don't want to lose what we have."

Kartik reached across the table, taking her hand in his.

Kartik: "You're not going to lose me. We'll stay connected, and when you come back, we'll pick up right where we left off."

Arushi smiled, feeling reassured by his words.

Arushi: "You're right. I just need to focus on the present. But can I ask for your help? I'm going to need someone to keep me grounded while I'm away."

Kartik: "Absolutely! I'll be your cheerleader. Just promise me you won't get too caught up in the hustle and forget about us."

Arushi chuckled.

Arushi: "Deal! I promise to keep you updated, and we can have video calls regularly."

Kartik: "And I'll send you care packages. You'll feel my love even from miles away."

Arushi squeezed his hand, grateful for his support. The conversation lifted the weight off her shoulders.

Arushi: "Thank you, Kartik. I really appreciate you."

Kartik: "Anytime. So, when do you leave?"

Arushi: "In about two weeks. I need to finalize some paperwork and pack my things."

Kartik nodded, feeling a mix of pride for her and sadness for the impending distance. They spent the rest of the afternoon discussing her internship and their future plans, intertwining their dreams like threads in a tapestry.

The next day, Arushi was busy packing her belongings and preparing for her new adventure. She was excited but nervous, and her heart raced as she thought about leaving Kartik behind. As she sorted through her clothes, she found a note that her mother had written her before moving out for college. It read: "Life is about embracing change and seizing opportunities. Don't let fear hold you back."

Reading it made her feel more resolute. She quickly texted Kartik.

Arushi: Hey! I found a note from Mom. It made me think—I'm ready for this change!

Kartik replied almost instantly.

Kartik: That's the spirit! Embrace it, and I'll be right here cheering you on!

Over the next few days, they focused on enjoying their time together, making the most of each moment before Arushi's departure. They visited their favorite spots, laughed over silly memories, and shared their hopes for the future. One evening, while walking through a beautiful park, they found a quiet bench and sat down.

Kartik: "Do you remember when we first met? It feels like a lifetime ago."

Arushi: "How could I forget? You were such an introvert, sitting alone in the corner!"

Kartik: (laughing) "And you were so outgoing, chatting with everyone. I thought you wouldn't even notice me."

Arushi: "But here we are! I noticed you for a reason."

Kartik smiled, feeling a warmth spread through him.

Kartik: "I'm glad you did. You've brought so much light into my life."

Arushi: "And you've made me feel seen. I never thought I could be this happy."

They shared a comfortable silence, both lost in their thoughts. Suddenly, Arushi's phone buzzed, snapping them back to reality. It was a message from her new internship coordinator. She opened it, her eyes widening.

Arushi: "Kartik! They want me to start earlier than expected! I have to leave in just a few days!"

Kartik's heart dropped. He fought to keep his expression neutral.

Kartik: "Wow, that's... sudden."

Arushi: "I know! I'm excited, but I'm also panicking a bit."

Kartik: "It's okay to feel that way. Just remember, you're capable of handling whatever comes your way."

Arushi nodded, but anxiety crept into her voice.

Arushi: "What if I struggle? What if I can't keep up with everything?"

Kartik: "You're going to do great, Arushi. Trust yourself. And if you ever feel overwhelmed, you can always call me."

Arushi smiled, feeling reassured.

Arushi: "Thanks, Kartik. You're always there for me."

The following days passed in a whirlwind of excitement and goodbyes. Arushi packed her things, and each time she folded a piece of clothing, she felt a pang of sadness at the thought of leaving Kartik. On her last evening in town, they met at their café, where it all began.

Kartik: "So, this is it, huh? The end of one chapter and the start of another."

Arushi: "It feels surreal. I wish I could take you with me."

Kartik: "In spirit, I'll be right there with you. Just remember everything we've talked about. You're never alone."

They exchanged heartfelt promises and a deep embrace, lingering in the warmth of each other's presence. As they parted that night, Arushi felt a mixture of excitement and apprehension. She was stepping into the unknown, but with Kartik's unwavering support, she felt a glimmer of hope shining through her fears.

As she settled into her new city, she faced the challenges head-on, determined to succeed while keeping Kartik close in her heart. They stayed connected through calls and messages, sharing the highs and lows of their respective journeys.

But as days turned into weeks, Arushi began to notice the pressure of balancing her internship and her relationship with Kartik. The demands of her job were intense, and she often found herself working late into the night. There were times when she felt too exhausted to call Kartik, which weighed heavily on her conscience.

One night, after a particularly grueling day, she finally found a moment to call him. As soon as he picked up, she could hear the concern in his voice.

Kartik: "Hey, Arushi! How was your day?"

Arushi: (sighing) "Long. I'm still at the office, and I'm so tired."

Kartik: "You need to take care of yourself. Have you had dinner?"

Arushi: "No, I skipped it. Just trying to finish up some reports."

Kartik: "You can't keep doing this. I worry about you."

Arushi: "I know, I know. I'm sorry. I just want to prove myself."

Kartik: "You don't have to prove anything to anyone. You're already doing great. Just take a step back and breathe."

Arushi felt her heart swell with gratitude.

Arushi: "You always know what to say. Thank you for being patient with me."

Kartik: "Always. Remember, I'm here for you, no matter what."

As she hung up, Arushi felt a renewed sense of determination. She promised herself that she would prioritize her well-being while embracing the challenges of her internship. The next day, she made a conscious effort to communicate more with Kartik, sharing her struggles and victories. They began to share their daily experiences, making each other feel involved despite the distance.

CHAPTER SEVENTEEN

Adventures in Togetherness

The next morning, the sun filtered through the trees, casting dappled shadows on the ground as the group slowly emerged from their tents. Kartik stretched, taking in the fresh scent of pine and the soft sounds of nature waking up around them. He felt energized, a stark contrast to how he often felt in the busy city life.

Aniket was already up, poking at the embers of the campfire from the previous night.

Aniket: "Morning, sleepyheads! Who's ready for breakfast? I think we should have a feast to celebrate our night under the stars!"

Meera, rubbing her eyes, groaned softly.

Meera: "A feast sounds amazing, but first, I need coffee. You know I can't function without it."

Arushi emerged from her tent, her hair slightly tousled but a bright smile on her face.

Arushi: "Good morning, everyone! What's the plan for today?"

Kartik looked at her, feeling warmth spread through him.

Kartik: "I think a hearty breakfast is a great start, followed by a hike to the waterfall we heard about. What do you think?"

Aniket nodded enthusiastically.

Aniket: "Absolutely! I heard it's beautiful. We can take some photos and maybe even swim if it's warm enough."

Meera perked up at the mention of swimming.

Meera: "Count me in! But first, breakfast!"

They gathered around the campfire, making pancakes and toasting bread, the aroma filling the air. The morning was filled with laughter and playful banter as they enjoyed their meal together.

Kartik, watching Arushi laugh at Aniket's jokes, felt a rush of happiness. After breakfast, they packed their bags and set out for the waterfall. The hike was filled with excitement as they shared stories and teased one another.

As they walked, Kartik found himself walking alongside Arushi, their shoulders brushing against each other.

Kartik: "I've been thinking a lot about what we talked about last night. You know, about being extraordinary."

Arushi looked at him curiously.

Arushi: "Oh? What's on your mind?"

Kartik paused, choosing his words carefully.

Kartik: "I used to believe that to be extraordinary, I needed to achieve big things or stand out in a crowd. But now, I realize that it's the small, genuine moments that truly define us. Like this trip, being here with you all."

Arushi smiled, her eyes sparkling.

Arushi: "That's a beautiful perspective, Kartik. It's the connections we make that matter the most. They enrich our lives and give them meaning."

Just then, they reached a clearing, and the sound of rushing water filled the air. The waterfall tumbled down the rocks, creating a misty spray that sparkled in the sunlight.

Aniket and Meera rushed ahead, excited to see the view.

Aniket: "This is incredible! Come on, let's get closer!"

Kartik and Arushi followed, their hearts racing with excitement. As they reached the edge of the water, the sight was breathtaking—the waterfall cascading into a crystal-clear pool, surrounded by vibrant greenery.

Meera squealed with delight.

Meera: "This is the perfect spot for a photo! Everyone, come over here!"

They all gathered by the water's edge, posing with the waterfall in the background. Aniket took the photo, capturing their joyful expressions. As the camera clicked, Kartik felt a surge of gratitude for these moments.

After the photo, Aniket and Meera wasted no time in changing into their swimsuits, diving into the water with splashes and laughter.

Aniket: "Come on in, the water is amazing!"

Kartik hesitated, feeling a bit shy, but Arushi took his hand, her grip reassuring.

Arushi: "Let's do it together! It'll be fun, I promise."

With a deep breath, Kartik nodded, and they both jumped into the water, laughter erupting as the cold water enveloped them. It was exhilarating, and for a moment, all worries faded away.

After swimming and playing in the water, they settled on the warm rocks to dry off. The sun bathed them in warmth, and the sound of the waterfall was soothing.

As they relaxed, Meera turned to Kartik, her expression serious.

Meera: "You know, Kartik, you have this quiet strength that people often overlook. Don't ever doubt your worth."

Kartik looked surprised, glancing at Arushi, who nodded in agreement.

Arushi: "She's right. Your kindness and the way you care for others is what makes you extraordinary."

Feeling encouraged, Kartik decided to be more open about his feelings.

Kartik: "Thank you, both of you. I really appreciate that. I've realized that it's important to surround ourselves with people who lift us up."

Aniket, lounging nearby, chimed in with a grin.

Aniket: "And don't forget to believe in yourself, buddy! You've got a great heart and so much to offer."

Kartik took a deep breath, his heart pounding as he looked at Arushi.

Kartik: "Speaking of believing, I want to make a promise. I want to be someone who isn't afraid to show who I really am. To live authentically, just like you all do."

Arushi's eyes softened, and she leaned closer to him.

Arushi: "That's a wonderful promise, Kartik. And I'll be here to support you every step of the way."

Kartik felt a rush of emotion, knowing he had a solid support system.

Kartik: "Thank you. I promise to cherish this friendship and all of you."

As the sun began to set, painting the sky in warm hues, they shared stories and laughter, making memories that would last a lifetime. Kartik felt a sense of belonging that he had longed for, and he knew this trip was more than just an adventure; it was the beginning of a beautiful journey with Arushi and their friends.

The Ripple Effect

As summer progressed, Arushi settled into her internship, which proved to be both exhilarating and exhausting. Each day brought new challenges and learning experiences, yet she often found herself longing for the familiar comfort of Kartik's presence. Their calls became her lifeline, but as the weeks passed, she felt a growing distance—not just in miles, but in emotions too.

One evening, as she wrapped up her work, she noticed a missed call from Kartik. Her heart sank a little. They had talked less frequently, and she had sensed a shift in his tone during their conversations. Picking up her phone, she dialed him back, hoping to bridge the gap.

Kartik: "Hey, I was just thinking about you! How's everything going?"

Arushi: "Hey! It's been hectic. I feel like I'm in a constant race against time."

Kartik: "I get that. Just remember to breathe. How's the work?"

Arushi: "Challenging, but good. I'm learning a lot. I just wish I had more time to unwind."

Kartik: "I know what you mean. It feels like we're both caught up in our own worlds. I miss our late-night talks."

Arushi hesitated, sensing the unspoken concern in his voice.

Arushi: "I miss them too. It's just... everything's been overwhelming lately."

Kartik: "You're doing amazing, Arushi. But don't forget about us. I want to hear about your day, not just the work stuff."

Arushi felt a pang of guilt. She had been so focused on her internship that she hadn't prioritized their connection.

Arushi: "You're right. I'll do better. Let's make time for each other. Can we schedule a call every few days?"

Kartik: "That sounds good. I just don't want you to feel alone in this."

Arushi: "I appreciate that. You have no idea how much your support means to me."

As they continued talking, Arushi felt the familiar warmth of their connection slowly wrapping around her, easing her worries. They exchanged stories, jokes, and laughter, and for a moment, she forgot about the pressures of her internship.

However, as the conversation drew to a close, Kartik's tone shifted again.

Kartik: "So, how's everything else? Are you making friends?"

Arushi: "Yeah, a few. But it's different here. Everyone is focused on their careers, and sometimes I feel a bit lost."

Kartik: "Just be yourself. You'll find your tribe. And if you ever need me to come visit, just say the word."

Arushi smiled at the thought.

Arushi: "That would be amazing! I'd love to show you around. But for now, let's plan our next call."

In the following days, Arushi worked hard to balance her responsibilities while nurturing her relationship with Kartik. She made it a point to share her little victories and challenges, ensuring that he felt involved in her life. They began to establish a routine of evening video calls, which filled her with joy and comfort. Yet, the emotional distance still lingered, as Kartik faced his own struggles back home.

One afternoon, after a particularly challenging week at her internship, Arushi received a text from Kartik.

Kartik: Hey, can we talk?

Arushi: Sure! Is everything okay?

Kartik: I've been feeling a bit off lately. Can we chat later tonight?

Arushi's heart raced as she read the message. She couldn't shake off the feeling that something deeper was brewing. That evening, as they connected over video, the tension was palpable.

Kartik: "Hey. Thanks for making time."

Arushi: "Of course! What's on your mind?"

Kartik took a deep breath, his eyes reflecting uncertainty.

Kartik: "I've been thinking a lot about us. About how things have changed since you moved."

Arushi felt a knot form in her stomach.

Arushi: "I know what you mean. It's been hard trying to juggle everything."

Kartik: "It's not just the distance. I feel like we're drifting. Like I'm losing you to this new life."

Arushi's heart sank, and she quickly reassured him.

Arushi: "You're not losing me, Kartik! I'm still here, just trying to adapt to everything."

Kartik: "I understand, but it's tough. I miss you. I miss us."

Arushi's eyes brimmed with tears.

Arushi: "I miss you too. It's been a struggle to adjust, and I never wanted you to feel this way."

Kartik: "Then let's change that. We need to prioritize each other. Maybe I can come visit you? We could spend a weekend together and reconnect."

Arushi felt a rush of excitement mixed with apprehension.

Arushi: "I'd love that! But what about your commitments here?"

Kartik shrugged, looking determined.

Kartik: "I can manage it. We need this, don't we?"

Arushi nodded, her heart swelling with gratitude.

Arushi: "Yes, we do. Let's make it happen."

As they discussed the logistics of Kartik's visit, Arushi felt a renewed sense of hope. They were not just surviving the distance but actively fighting for their relationship. With every passing moment, they reaffirmed their commitment to one another, igniting a flame that had begun to flicker in the face of challenges.

Days later, the anticipation built as Kartik's visit drew closer. Arushi could hardly concentrate on work, her mind swirling with excitement about the moments they would share. She envisioned exploring the city together, visiting local spots, and simply enjoying each other's company. However, she also felt a flicker of anxiety. Would things feel the same after all this time apart?

The day finally arrived. Arushi stood at the bus station, her heart racing as she scanned the crowd for any sign of Kartik. Just then, she spotted him, his familiar figure stepping off the bus. He looked around, his face lighting up when their eyes met.

Arushi: (running towards him) "Kartik!"

He opened his arms, and she jumped into his embrace, feeling a rush of warmth and familiarity wash over her.

Kartik: "It's so good to see you!"

Arushi pulled back slightly, searching his eyes.

Arushi: "You're here! I can't believe it!"

Kartik laughed, brushing his hair back.

Kartik: "I wouldn't miss this for the world."

They spent the afternoon exploring the city, visiting iconic landmarks and sharing stories about their lives since the last time they had seen each other. Laughter echoed through the streets as they reminisced about their time together, and for a moment, it felt like no time had passed at all.

That evening, as they sat on a bench overlooking the sunset, Kartik turned to Arushi, a serious expression on his face.

Kartik: "This has been perfect, but I need to talk to you about something."

Arushi's heart raced at the change in his tone.

Arushi: "What is it?"

Kartik hesitated, taking a deep breath.

Kartik: "I've been thinking about our future. About where we want this relationship to go."

Arushi felt a rush of emotions at his words.

Arushi: "Me too. I want us to last, Kartik. But how do we make that happen?"

Kartik smiled, relieved by her response.

Kartik: "I think we need to be more intentional about our time together, even when we're apart. And when I graduate, I want to explore opportunities in your city. I want us to build a future together."

Arushi felt her heart soar at his words.

Arushi: "Really? You would do that?"

Kartik: "Of course. I believe in us."

Tears welled in Arushi's eyes as she took his hand.

Arushi: "You have no idea how much that means to me. I want us to build a life together too."

As the sun dipped below the horizon, casting a golden hue over them, Arushi and Kartik felt a renewed sense of commitment. The challenges ahead seemed less daunting, knowing they would face them together. Their hearts, once fluttering with uncertainty, now beat in unison as they envisioned a future filled with love, dreams, and the promise of togetherness.

CHAPTER NINETEEN

The Promise of Tomorrow

Setting: The park, where Kartik and Arushi often meet. The sun is setting, casting a golden hue over the landscape.

Kartik: (sitting on a bench, looking at the sunset) "You know, Arushi, every time I see a sunset, I think about how beautiful it is to have a new day ahead. Just like our journey."

Arushi: (smiling) "That's a lovely thought, Kartik. Each day brings new possibilities. It's like a fresh canvas waiting for us to paint it with our dreams."

Kartik: (turning to her, serious) "I want to paint our canvas together, Arushi. I want to create a future that's bright and filled with love."

Arushi: (softly) "I feel the same way. But sometimes, I wonder if I deserve this happiness. It feels surreal."

Kartik: (taking her hands) "You deserve every bit of happiness, Arushi. Don't doubt it for a second. Remember what we talked about? It's not about how we look; it's about the hearts we carry."

Arushi: (nodding) "You're right. Your words always bring me back to reality. It's just... sometimes I fear what lies ahead."

Kartik: "Fear is normal, but we shouldn't let it hold us back. We have each other, and that's what matters. Together, we can face anything."

Arushi: (smiling through her fears) "Together."

Kartik: "Exactly! And speaking of together, how about we make a promise?"

Arushi: (curiously) "A promise?"

Kartik: "Yes. A promise that no matter what challenges come our way, we'll face them together. That we'll always be honest and support each other."

Arushi: "I love that idea. It's like a bond that we're creating, one that will keep us strong."

Kartik: (grinning) "So, do we have a deal?"

Arushi: (enthusiastically) "Absolutely! I promise to always be there for you, and I expect the same from you."

Kartik: (with a twinkle in his eyes) "I promise, Arushi. I am ordinary by looks, but extraordinary by heart. And I'll always choose you."

Arushi: (leaning closer) "And I'll always choose you too, Kartik. You have no idea how much that means to me."

Kartik: "We'll create our story, Arushi. One filled with laughter, challenges, love, and endless adventures."

Arushi: "I can't wait to see what tomorrow brings. Together."

Kartik: (as the sun dips below the horizon) "Together."

CHAPTER TWENTY

A Promise of Adventures

A few days later, at a local café where Kartik and Arushi have come to celebrate a small milestone in their relationship. Aniket and Meera join them.

Arushi: (stirring her coffee) "I can't believe it's been a month since we made that promise. Time flies, doesn't it?"

Kartik: (smiling) "It really does! Each day feels like a new adventure with you."

Aniket: (leaning back in his chair) "And it's only just the beginning! What's next on your agenda, lovebirds?"

Meera: (grinning) "Yeah, spill the beans! I hope it involves more than just sitting here and being cute!"

Kartik: (chuckling) "Well, I was thinking we could go hiking this weekend. There's a beautiful trail about an hour away. What do you guys think?"

Aniket: (perking up) "Count me in! I love a good hike. Plus, I could use some time outdoors."

Meera: (nodding enthusiastically) "Same here! It'll be a great chance for us all to hang out. I'm in!"

Arushi: (smiling at Kartik) "See? It's a perfect plan! Just the four of us, surrounded by nature."

Kartik: "Exactly! Just imagine the fun we'll have."

Aniket: "And the pictures! We need some epic shots to document our adventure."

Meera: "Oh, I can already picture it. Kartik struggling to keep up while Arushi sprints ahead!"

Kartik: (teasingly) "Hey! I'll surprise you with my stamina! Just wait and see."

Arushi: (playfully) "But you better keep up! I've been practicing my hiking skills."

Aniket: "No worries, Kartik. I'll make sure to motivate you. Maybe we can race!"

Meera: (laughs) "I can already see the chaos unfolding. But remember, if you fall behind, I might just leave you behind!"

Kartik: (laughing) "So, it's a plan to ditch me, huh? I'll make sure to keep pace then!"

Arushi: (with a thoughtful expression) "Kartik, can I ask you something?"

Kartik: "Of course. What's on your mind?"

Arushi: "What if we face challenges that test our promise? What if things don't go as we hope?"

Aniket: (serious for a moment) "That's a good question. But every journey has its bumps. It's how we deal with them that counts."

Meera: "Exactly! Just keep communicating. That's the key to any relationship."

Kartik: (taking Arushi's hands) "Then we face them together, just like we promised. Every relationship has its ups and downs. What matters is how we choose to navigate those moments."

Arushi: "You're right. I just want us to stay strong, no matter what."

Kartik: "We will. Our connection is built on trust, understanding, and love. As long as we communicate and support each other, we can overcome anything."

Aniket: "And remember, we're all here for each other. Friends stick together."

Meera: (smiling warmly) "That's what friendship is for! We'll cheer you on every step of the way."

Arushi: (raising her coffee cup) "To us and our journey ahead!"

Kartik: (clinking his cup with hers) "To us!"

Aniket: "And to unforgettable adventures!"

Meera: "Cheers to friendship, love, and all the memories we'll create together!"

CHAPTER TWENTY-ONE

Bridges of Trust

Setting: A few days after their café meetup, Kartik, Arushi, Aniket, and Meera embark on their hiking trip. As they trek through the scenic forest trail, the fresh air and camaraderie lighten the mood.

Meera: (giggling as she playfully shoves Aniket) "Come on, slowpoke! I thought you were the hiking pro."

Aniket: (mocking) "I'm just giving you a head start, Meera. I don't want you feeling bad when I overtake you."

Kartik: (walking beside Arushi, a bit out of breath) "This was a great idea... but I didn't think it would be this exhausting."

Arushi: (smirking) "I told you to work on your stamina. But you're doing fine, don't worry."

Kartik: "I'm trying to keep up. But this view... makes it all worth it."

Aniket: (shouting from a few steps ahead) "Kartik! Keep going, man! You got this!"

Meera: "Yeah, you can't let Arushi outshine you now!"

Kartik: (laughing while panting) "Oh, I see how it is. A competition now, is it?"

Arushi: (smiling) "No competition, just support. You're doing great."

As they continue their hike, the group eventually reaches the peak of the trail—a beautiful, open view of the valley below.

Arushi: (looking at the view, awed) "Wow. This is... breathtaking."

Kartik: (catching his breath, gazing at Arushi's expression instead of the view) "It really is."

Meera: (sitting down on a nearby rock) "This is why I love hiking. The reward is always worth the struggle."

Aniket: (nodding) "Life lesson right there. The tougher the climb, the sweeter the view."

Kartik: (sitting next to Arushi, voice softer) "Just like in life. The more challenges we face, the stronger we get. Right?"

Arushi: (smiling at Kartik) "Exactly. Every step forward brings us closer to something beautiful."

Meera: (teasing) "Okay, philosophers. Enough deep talk! Let's enjoy this moment."

Aniket: (laughing) "Yeah, before Meera starts preaching about 'the meaning of the journey'."

The group shares a laugh, but as they rest, Kartik and Arushi find themselves lost in their own quiet moment, the weight of unspoken promises between them.

Kartik: (turning to Arushi, voice thoughtful) "You know, there's something I wanted to say... something that's been on my mind."

Arushi: (raising an eyebrow) "What is it?"

Kartik: (after a pause, gathering his courage) "I know I'm not the most outgoing or impressive guy around. But... I am who I am. And, if you can accept that, I'll give you everything I have. I'm ordinary by looks, but extraordinary by heart. Will you be my forever?"

Arushi's expression softens, and for a moment, time seems to stop.

Arushi: (smiling warmly) "I wouldn't want anything more than that, Kartik. Yes, I will."

As they exchange a look filled with emotion, Aniket and Meera, noticing the shift, look at each other knowingly but say nothing. They understand this is a moment meant for just the two of them.

Aniket: (breaking the silence with a grin) "Alright, you two. Time to head back before it gets dark. We still have the trek down."

Meera: (playfully) "And Kartik still has to prove his stamina on the way back."

Kartik: (laughing) "Don't worry, I'm ready. I have all the motivation I need now."

As they begin their descent, Kartik and Arushi walk side by side, hands brushing occasionally, knowing that their journey together has only just begun.

Quote of the Day: "In every uphill climb, we find strength we never knew we had, and at the summit, we discover the beauty of the journey."

CHAPTER TWENTY-TWO

Threads of Connection

Setting: Back at the city, the next few days are filled with excitement as Kartik and Arushi navigate their newfound relationship. They decide to meet for dinner at a cozy restaurant to talk about their future.

Arushi: (sipping her drink, a playful smile on her face) "So, what's the first thing on our agenda as a couple?"

Kartik: (grinning back) "Well, I was thinking we should tackle the mystery of how to make the best pasta together. What do you say?"

Arushi: (laughing) "Are you sure you're ready for that challenge? I might just end up being the master chef."

Kartik: (feigning seriousness) "Challenge accepted. But if I burn the kitchen down, you're responsible for putting out the fire!"

As their laughter fills the air, Aniket and Meera enter the restaurant. They spot Kartik and Arushi and approach their table.

Aniket: (playfully) "Well, look who's getting cozy! Didn't know dinner dates were on the agenda!"

Meera: (teasing) "You two seem like you're in your own little world. Should we interrupt?"

Kartik and Arushi exchange amused glances before Arushi responds.

Arushi: "Not at all! Join us! We were just discussing our culinary plans."

Aniket: (smirking) "Culinary plans? Sounds serious. So, when is the cooking competition?"

Kartik: (smiling) "As soon as we figure out how to not set off the smoke alarms."

Meera: (giggling) "I'll bring the fire extinguisher, just in case."

As the four friends settle into a comfortable conversation, Arushi feels a sense of warmth and belonging. Their friendship has always been the foundation, but now it's evolving into something more profound.

Arushi: (leaning into the conversation) "So, what's new with you two? Any exciting adventures on the horizon?"

Aniket: (enthusiastically) "Well, I've been thinking about planning a weekend trip. Just us four—somewhere we can hike and explore!"

Meera: (nodding) "I'm in! Fresh air, great company, and maybe a few campfire stories."

Kartik: (looking at Arushi) "What do you think? A weekend escape sounds perfect, right?"

Arushi: (smiling brightly) "Absolutely! Count me in. I can't wait for the adventure."

The conversation flows easily, with shared stories and laughter echoing throughout the restaurant. As they finish their meals, Kartik feels a growing desire to express his feelings to Arushi in a more profound way.

Kartik: (clearing his throat, looking a bit nervous) "Hey, can we take a moment for something serious?"

Meera: (leaning in, curious) "Oh, this sounds interesting. What's on your mind?"

Arushi: (her expression shifts to attentive) "What is it, Kartik?"

He takes a deep breath, feeling the weight of the moment.

Kartik: "I just wanted to say... having you all here tonight, it makes me realize how much I value our friendships. Arushi, you mean so much to me. I want to build a future with you, filled with adventures and laughter."

Arushi blushes, her heart fluttering at Kartik's words.

Arushi: (softly) "I feel the same way, Kartik. I'm so grateful to have you in my life. Together, we can create something beautiful."

Aniket: (grinning widely) "Aw, look at them! This is what friendship is all about—supporting each other through thick and thin."

Meera: (mockingly wiping a tear) "It's so beautiful, it's making me emotional! Just promise us you won't become one of those mushy couples."

The group bursts into laughter, lightening the mood again.

Kartik: (smirking) "No mushiness here, just adventure and pasta disasters!"

As they finish their dinner, a sense of excitement fills the air. They start planning their weekend trip, weaving dreams of hiking, cooking over campfires, and sharing stories under the stars.

Quote of the Day: "True friendship is like a bridge—strong enough to withstand the storms of life and beautiful enough to appreciate the journey together."

4o mini

CHAPTER TWENTY-THREE

Into the Wilderness

Setting: The weekend has arrived, and the four friends embark on their much-anticipated trip. They drive to a nearby national park, the excitement palpable as they approach the scenic landscape filled with towering trees and winding trails.

Aniket: (glancing out the window) "Look at that view! I can already feel the adventure in the air."

Meera: (snapping a photo with her phone) "This is Instagram gold! Nature at its finest."

Arushi: (smiling, taking in the scenery) "I can't wait to hit the trails. This is exactly what we need—fresh air and some time away from the city."

Kartik: (focusing on the road, smiling) "And some quality time together. Let's make it unforgettable."

After parking the car, they gather their backpacks and gear, excitement bubbling as they prepare for their hike.

Aniket: (strapping on his backpack) "Alright, team! Let's do a quick check—snacks, water, and of course, the firestarter for later."

Meera: (playfully rolling her eyes) "Always the planner, Aniket. I'm just here for the snacks!"

As they step onto the trail, the sound of crunching leaves underfoot fills the air. The path leads them deeper into the forest, surrounded by lush greenery and the sweet scent of pine.

Kartik: (pointing ahead) "How about we take that trail to the left? It looks less traveled, and I love a good adventure."

Arushi: (nodding eagerly) "Yes! I love exploring new paths. Let's go!"

As they walk, they share stories, laughter echoing through the trees. Kartik feels a growing sense of belonging, especially with Arushi by his side.

Meera: (turning to Arushi) "So, how do you feel about Kartik now that you're officially a couple?"

Arushi: (grinning) "I feel like I'm in a dream. He's just so genuine and supportive. It's refreshing."

Aniket: (teasingly) "Don't let it go to your head, Kartik! You still have to impress us with your cooking skills later."

Kartik chuckles, feeling more at ease.

Kartik: "I promise not to burn the pasta! It's going to be a culinary masterpiece."

After hiking for a while, they stop at a scenic overlook. The view is breathtaking—rolling hills stretch into the distance, kissed by the warm afternoon sun.

Arushi: (taking a deep breath) "This is beautiful. It makes all the hustle and bustle of the city worth it."

Meera: (leaning on the railing) "We should take a group photo here. This moment deserves to be captured!"

They gather together, arms around each other, grinning widely as Meera snaps a few pictures.

Aniket: (playfully) "Now, everyone say 'Friendship!' on the count of three!"

All: "One, two, three—Friendship!"

The camera clicks, freezing the moment in time. As they finish up, they sit on the grass, enjoying the snacks they packed.

Kartik: (biting into a granola bar) "So, what's next on our adventure list? More hiking or should we head back to set up camp?"

Arushi: (thoughtfully) "I'd love to hike a bit more, but I'm also eager to try cooking over a campfire. That's part of the experience, right?"

Aniket and Meera nod in agreement, their eyes sparkling with anticipation.

Aniket: "Let's do a quick hike and then head back to camp. We can collect some firewood on the way!"

As they pack up and continue their hike, the bond between them deepens. They share stories from their past, revealing dreams and fears that draw them closer together.

Meera: (leaning closer to Arushi) "I'm so happy for you two. It's nice to see you so in sync with Kartik."

Arushi: (blushing slightly) "Thanks, Meera. He really makes me feel special."

As they wrap up their hike, they begin the trek back to their campsite, hearts full of joy and laughter.

Kartik: (with a playful glint in his eyes) "Okay, who's ready to witness my culinary skills?"

As they reach their campsite, they set up the area for their evening feast under the stars. An excitement fills the air, the promise of friendship, laughter, and a beautiful night ahead.

Quote of the Day: "In the wilderness, we discover not just the beauty of nature but the strength of our connections."

4o mini

CHAPTER TWENTY-FOUR

The Heart of the Forest

The following morning, the group woke up to the sound of birds chirping and sunlight streaming through the trees. They decided to go on a hike, eager to explore the wilderness.

As they walked, Kartik and Arushi stayed close, their hands brushing against each other occasionally.

Arushi: "Isn't it amazing how peaceful it is here? It's like the world just fades away."

Kartik smiled, feeling content.

Kartik: "Yeah, it's nice to disconnect from everything. Just us, nature, and... well, the occasional wildlife."

Aniket, who was ahead, turned around with a grin.

Aniket: "Hey, don't forget about me! I'm the adventure leader here!"

Meera laughed, pulling out her camera.

Meera: "Let's capture this moment! Everyone, say 'nature'!"

They all posed, the laughter echoing through the trees as Meera snapped the picture. After some time, they found a beautiful clearing by a river. The water sparkled in the sunlight, and the sound of flowing water created a serene atmosphere.

Arushi sighed happily as she approached the riverbank.

Arushi: "This is perfect! Let's take a break here."

Kartik followed her, his heart racing as he watched her excitement.

Kartik: "Should we have a small picnic?"

Aniket and Meera agreed, and soon they were spread out on a blanket, sharing sandwiches and snacks. The atmosphere was filled with lighthearted banter and laughter.

As they finished eating, Arushi looked at Kartik, her expression serious.

Arushi: "Kartik, can I ask you something?"

Kartik's heart skipped a beat.

Kartik: "Of course! What's on your mind?"

Arushi hesitated, her brow furrowing slightly.

Arushi: "Do you think we can maintain our connection even when things get busy? I know we both have big dreams ahead."

Kartik nodded, feeling a sense of determination.

Kartik: "I believe we can. We'll make time for each other, no matter what. Our bond is strong enough."

Meera chimed in, her voice light-hearted.

Meera: "And besides, I'll make sure you both schedule regular catch-ups. No slacking off!"

They all laughed, and the tension eased. As the afternoon wore on, they decided to explore the area, wandering further into the woods.

Kartik found himself walking alongside Arushi, their shoulders brushing against each other.

Kartik: "I've really enjoyed this trip. It's reminded me of what truly matters."

Arushi smiled, her eyes sparkling.

Arushi: "Me too. Sometimes we need to step back to see what we're really fighting for."

CHAPTER TWENTY-FIVE

Whispers of the Wind

As the sun began to set, painting the sky in shades of purple and gold, the group found themselves in a picturesque spot, surrounded by tall trees swaying gently in the breeze. Kartik felt a sense of peace enveloping them as they took in the beauty around them.

Aniket, full of energy, broke the serene silence.

Aniket: "Who's ready for a little adventure? Let's climb that hill over there! I bet the view from the top is incredible."

Meera, who had been snapping pictures, looked up from her camera.

Meera: "That sounds like a great idea! Let's do it!"

Kartik exchanged a glance with Arushi, who smiled and nodded, her excitement evident.

Kartik: "Alright then! Let's go see what's waiting for us at the top."

As they climbed, Kartik found himself walking beside Arushi, their conversation flowing effortlessly.

Kartik: "You know, I've always loved being in nature. It makes me feel alive, like anything is possible."

Arushi turned to him, her eyes thoughtful.

Arushi: "I feel the same way. It's as if the worries of the world just vanish. I wish we could bottle up this feeling."

Finally reaching the top of the hill, they all paused to catch their breath. The view was breathtaking; rolling hills stretched out before them, with the river glistening like a silver ribbon below.

Aniket threw his arms wide open, embracing the moment.

Aniket: "This is what I'm talking about! Look at this view! It's epic!"

Meera took a deep breath, capturing the scene with her camera.

Meera: "I'm definitely posting this. #NatureLovers."

Kartik stood quietly, absorbing the beauty around him. He turned to Arushi, who was staring out at the horizon, her expression contemplative.

Kartik: "What are you thinking about?"

Arushi hesitated before speaking, her voice soft.

Arushi: "I was just thinking how precious moments like these are. They remind us to appreciate life and the people in it."

Kartik nodded, his heart swelling with emotion.

Kartik: "You're right. I want to make sure we never lose sight of this connection."

Aniket and Meera joined them, interrupting the moment.

Aniket: "Enough of the mushy stuff! Let's take a group photo before the sun sets!"

They all gathered together, posing with the stunning backdrop. Meera clicked the picture, capturing their laughter and camaraderie. As the sun dipped below the horizon, the air grew cooler, and they started their descent back to the campsite.

Later that evening, they sat around the campfire, the crackling flames casting flickering shadows on their faces. The air was filled with the smell of roasting marshmallows, and the sound of their laughter echoed through the trees.

Kartik glanced at Arushi, who was smiling as she toasted a marshmallow.

Kartik: "So, what's next on our adventure list? More camping? Hiking?"

Meera chimed in, her eyes sparkling.

Meera: "How about a night hike? I've heard the stars are breathtaking away from the city lights."

Aniket nodded enthusiastically.

Aniket: "Count me in! I want to see the Milky Way!"

Arushi looked at Kartik, her eyes reflecting the firelight.

Arushi: "What do you think, Kartik? Are you up for a little adventure in the dark?"

Kartik grinned, feeling brave.

Kartik: "Absolutely! As long as I have you all with me, I'm in."

CHAPTER TWENTY-SIX

Beneath the Stars

After finishing their snacks, they geared up for the night hike, grabbing flashlights and extra layers. The night was cool, and the air felt electric with excitement.

As they walked along the trail, the moonlight illuminated their path, and the sounds of the forest surrounded them. Aniket led the way, his flashlight beam cutting through the darkness.

Kartik walked closely beside Arushi, their hands brushing against each other occasionally.

Kartik: "Isn't it amazing how different everything looks at night?"

Arushi nodded, her eyes wide with wonder.

Arushi: "It's like the world transforms into something magical."

They reached a clearing where the stars shone brightly above them, more vivid than they had ever seen. Everyone stopped, captivated by the beauty of the night sky.

Meera pointed upwards, her voice filled with awe.

Meera: "Look at that! You can see the Milky Way!"

Aniket pulled out his phone, eager to capture the moment.

Aniket: "This is going straight to Instagram. You all are going to be so jealous of this view!"

As they lay on the grass, gazing up at the stars, Kartik turned to Arushi, feeling the weight of the moment.

Kartik: "Arushi, do you ever wonder what else is out there? Beyond the stars, I mean?"

Arushi looked at him, her expression thoughtful.

Arushi: "All the time. I think about how small we are in the grand scheme of things, but also how connected we are. It's a beautiful contradiction."

Kartik felt a pull towards her, the intensity of the moment filling him with a sense of purpose.

Kartik: "You know, I used to think that being ordinary was a limitation. But now, I realize it's my heart that makes me extraordinary."

Arushi turned to him, her eyes shining.

Arushi: "And that's what makes you so special, Kartik. You have a kind heart, and that's more important than anything else."

The air felt charged with unspoken emotions as they shared a lingering glance. Aniket and Meera were joking nearby, but in that moment, it was just the two of them beneath the stars.

Kartik took a deep breath, feeling the urge to share more.

Kartik: "You've changed my perspective on life, Arushi. Being with you makes me want to be better."

Arushi smiled, her cheeks flushing slightly.

Arushi: "And you inspire me, Kartik. You remind me that it's okay to be vulnerable and authentic."

The night continued with laughter and stories, but for Kartik and Arushi, it was a turning point—a moment that solidified their connection. As they made their way back to the campsite, Kartik couldn't shake the feeling that this trip was just the beginning of something extraordinary.

CHAPTER TWENTY-SEVEN

The Heart of the Matter

The evening settled in, and the group returned to their campsite, still buzzing with the energy of the day. A warm fire crackled in the center, providing a cozy glow as they gathered around. Aniket began to roast marshmallows, while Meera, still energetic, shared the stories of their hikes.

Arushi sat beside Kartik, their knees brushing occasionally. He stole glances at her, captivated by her genuine smile and the way her laughter lit up the space around them.

Kartik: "This day was incredible. I never expected to feel so free and happy."

Arushi looked at him, her expression softening.

Arushi: "I'm glad you enjoyed it. It's nice to escape the hustle and bustle of city life and just be ourselves."

Kartik nodded, gathering the courage to share more of his thoughts.

Kartik: "You know, being here with all of you makes me realize how important it is to have a strong support system. I've spent so much time worrying about fitting in, but this... this feels right."

Meera, overhearing their conversation, chimed in while toasting another marshmallow.

Meera: "That's because we're all here for each other. It's about authenticity, right? Not just putting on a facade."

Aniket grinned, taking a bite of his perfectly toasted marshmallow.

Aniket: "Exactly! And Kartik, you've got to be yourself. Look at you now—embracing adventure and letting go of those insecurities."

Kartik felt warmth spreading through him at his friends' words. He appreciated their support more than he could express.

Kartik: "Thanks, guys. I want to keep this momentum going, you know? Not just for myself but for all of us."

As the night grew darker, they began sharing stories around the fire—tales of childhood, dreams, and fears. Kartik found himself sharing more than he ever had before, his heart feeling lighter with every word.

Arushi leaned closer, her interest evident.

Arushi: "What about your dreams, Kartik? What do you really want to do?"

Kartik hesitated, feeling vulnerable but ready to open up.

Kartik: "Honestly? I've always wanted to create something meaningful, something that could help others. Maybe write a book, or even start a community project."

Aniket's eyes lit up.

Aniket: "That's a fantastic idea! You should totally go for it. I can see you doing something amazing."

Meera nodded enthusiastically.

Meera: "And I'd help too! We could organize something together, raise awareness or support a cause. Count me in!"

Feeling encouraged, Kartik smiled.

Kartik: "I appreciate that. It's been a dream of mine for a long time, but I always felt it was out of reach. Now, with your support, I feel like it's possible."

Arushi looked at him with admiration.

Arushi: "You've already taken the first step by being open about it. That's a huge achievement in itself."

As the fire crackled, casting a warm glow around them, Kartik felt a profound sense of connection. He turned to Arushi, his heart racing.

Kartik: "Arushi, there's something I need to tell you. You've inspired me to be more than I thought I could be. I've realized that what truly matters is to be honest with myself and those I care about."

She looked back at him, her eyes sparkling in the firelight.

Arushi: "I'm so glad to hear that, Kartik. You're already extraordinary by heart."

Taking a deep breath, Kartik spoke from his heart.

Kartik: "I may be ordinary in looks, but I want to be extraordinary in who I am. Will you support me on this journey?"

The moment hung in the air, charged with sincerity and hope. Arushi smiled warmly.

Arushi: "Always. You're not just ordinary, Kartik. You're capable of incredible things, and I'll be right by your side."

Aniket, sensing the deep connection between them, teased lightly.

Aniket: "Look at that! My best friend is falling in love with life and maybe someone special."

Kartik felt a rush of warmth at Aniket's words, glancing at Arushi, who blushed slightly.

Kartik: "I'm just grateful to have you all in my life."

The night wore on, and the stars twinkled above them like diamonds scattered across a velvet sky. They shared stories and dreams, weaving a tapestry of friendship that felt unbreakable.

As the fire began to die down, Kartik felt a sense of peace envelop him. He was exactly where he needed to be—surrounded by friends who believed in him and shared his journey.

Before they turned in for the night, Aniket proposed one last idea.

Aniket: "Let's make a promise. We'll all write down one goal we want to achieve this year, and when we meet again, we'll share our progress."

Meera nodded enthusiastically.

Meera: "I love that idea! It'll keep us motivated."

Kartik smiled, feeling excited about the prospect.

Kartik: "I'm in! I want to write my first chapter of the book I've always dreamed of."

Arushi leaned in closer, her voice warm.

Arushi: "And I'll help you brainstorm ideas. Together, we can make this happen."

As they settled into their tents, Kartik's heart swelled with gratitude and hope. The promise of tomorrow felt bright, and he knew he was ready to embrace whatever came next. With friends by his side and dreams within reach, he was finally ready to step into the extraordinary life he had always desired.

CHAPTER TWENTY-EIGHT

New Beginnings

The morning sun spilled over the horizon, painting the campsite in warm hues of orange and gold. Birds chirped cheerfully, welcoming a new day as Kartik awoke to the sounds of laughter and the smell of breakfast wafting through the air. He rubbed his eyes and crawled out of his tent, feeling a mix of excitement and anticipation. Today marked the beginning of a new chapter in his life.

As he stretched and took in the fresh, crisp air, he spotted Aniket flipping pancakes over the fire, with Meera playfully trying to steal one before it hit the plate. Arushi sat nearby, sipping her coffee and observing the scene with a smile. Kartik couldn't help but smile too, feeling grateful for the friendship that surrounded him.

Kartik: "Morning, everyone! Smells amazing!"

Aniket: "Morning, sleepyhead! Get over here and grab a pancake before Meera eats them all!"

Meera: "Hey! I'm just helping with quality control! I wouldn't want you to get a bad one."

Kartik laughed as he joined them at the makeshift dining area, feeling a warmth in his heart as they all settled down together. The camaraderie felt tangible, and for the first time, he truly felt like he belonged.

As they enjoyed breakfast, the conversation flowed easily. They shared jokes and stories, and Aniket proposed an idea that sparked Kartik's interest.

Aniket: "How about we hike to the waterfall today? I hear it's beautiful, and we can do some swimming. What do you think?"

Meera: "I'm in! It sounds like a perfect way to end our camping trip. Plus, I need a little adventure before we head back to reality."

Kartik: "That sounds incredible. I've never been swimming in a natural waterfall before."

Arushi: "Neither have I! Let's make it happen. It'll be a great way to celebrate our new promises."

As they finished their breakfast, Kartik felt a sense of anticipation building inside him. Today was not just about hiking; it was about taking another step toward his dreams. He thought of his promise to write and how he wanted to share his journey with his friends.

After breakfast, they packed their bags, ensuring they had everything they needed for the hike. The excitement was palpable as they set off, the trail winding through lush greenery and vibrant wildflowers. They walked side by side, chatting about everything under the sun.

Meera: "I can't believe how fast this trip has gone. It feels like just yesterday we were planning it."

Aniket: "I know! But I think we've made some great memories. Who knew Kartik could be such a daredevil?"

Kartik chuckled, shaking his head.

Kartik: "I'm not a daredevil. I'm just embracing the moment."

Arushi smiled, glancing at him.

Arushi: "That's what I love about you, Kartik. You're willing to step out of your comfort zone."

As they reached a scenic overlook, they paused to catch their breath and take in the view. The landscape stretched out before them—a patchwork of green hills and valleys, with the distant sound of rushing water. Kartik felt a rush of inspiration, realizing that this was where he wanted to find his voice.

They continued their hike, the sounds of nature surrounding them. As they approached the waterfall, the air grew cooler, and the sound of cascading water became louder. Kartik felt a thrill of excitement as they finally reached their destination. The waterfall tumbled down from a rocky cliff, splashing into a clear pool below, creating a mist that sparkled in the sunlight.

Aniket: "This is breathtaking! Who's ready to jump in?"

Meera squealed in delight, running toward the water.

Meera: "I am! Come on, everyone!"

Kartik looked at Arushi, who was admiring the scene with wide eyes.

Kartik: "Are you ready?"

Arushi: "Absolutely! Let's do this!"

One by one, they shed their clothes and stepped into the cool, refreshing water. The laughter and joy echoed around them as they splashed each other and swam beneath the waterfall. Kartik felt liberated, his worries washing away with each wave.

As they floated in the pool, Aniket splashed water at Meera, who retaliated by splashing him back. The playful banter continued, but Kartik found himself drifting closer to Arushi. They exchanged glances, their hearts racing with unspoken feelings.

Kartik: "This is amazing, isn't it?"

Arushi: "It really is! I feel so free and alive right now."

Kartik: "I've never felt this way before. It's like I'm finally coming into my own."

Arushi smiled, her eyes sparkling with admiration.

Arushi: "You've always had it in you, Kartik. You just needed the right moment to let it shine."

Kartik's heart raced at her words. They shared a moment of understanding, a connection that felt deeper than friendship.

After swimming, they sat by the water's edge, letting the sun dry them off. Aniket and Meera were busy taking selfies, capturing their adventurous day. Kartik felt a sense of calm wash over him as he looked at Arushi, who was gazing at the waterfall.

Kartik: "Hey, Arushi?"

Arushi: "Yeah?"

Kartik: "I want to share something with you. Remember the promise we made last night?"

She turned to face him, curiosity evident in her expression.

Arushi: "Of course. What's on your mind?"

Kartik: "I've always wanted to write a book. It's been a dream of mine for a long time, but I've never really known where to start. Being here with you all has inspired me to finally take that leap."

Arushi's eyes lit up.

Arushi: "That's incredible, Kartik! You should definitely go for it. You have so many stories inside you waiting to be told."

Kartik took a deep breath, feeling more confident.

Kartik: "I want to write about our journey, our friendships, and the lessons we've learned. I want to show others that it's okay to be different and that true beauty lies within."

Arushi: "I love that idea. I can't wait to read it! You have such a unique perspective."

Encouraged by her words, Kartik continued.

Kartik: "I want to include all of you in my book. Your support means everything to me, and I want to celebrate our friendship."

Arushi beamed, her excitement contagious.

Arushi: "Count me in! I'd love to help however I can."

As they sat together by the waterfall, Kartik felt a renewed sense of purpose. The beauty of the moment was amplified by the bond he shared with his friends. He knew that this was just the beginning of a new chapter, not only in his life but in their collective journey.

Later, as they packed up to leave, Aniket called out.

Aniket: "Okay, everyone, before we head back, let's take one last group photo to remember this day!"

They gathered together, arms around each other, their smiles wide and genuine. The camera clicked, capturing the moment, and Kartik felt a wave of gratitude wash over him.

As they started their hike back to camp, the conversations flowed seamlessly. Kartik's heart was lighter than it had been in a long time. He knew he was surrounded by people who believed in him, and that made all the difference.

Meera: "You know, I've learned so much about myself on this trip. I think we all have."

Kartik: "Yeah, it's been a journey of self-discovery, for sure. I'm grateful to have you all by my side."

Arushi: "Here's to new beginnings and the adventures that lie ahead."

Kartik nodded, feeling a sense of excitement for what the future held. He was ready to embrace his dreams, and he knew that with his friends by his side, he could conquer anything.

As they reached the campsite, the sun began to set, casting a golden glow over the landscape. The day had been filled with laughter, reflection, and newfound aspirations, and Kartik felt a surge of inspiration.

They gathered around the fire once more, this time reflecting on their day and sharing their individual goals. Kartik listened intently, feeling more connected to his friends than ever before. It was as if they had forged an unbreakable bond that would carry them through whatever challenges lay ahead.

As they shared their thoughts and dreams, Kartik couldn't help but smile, knowing that this was just the beginning of something extraordinary. Together, they would support one another, embrace their individuality, and create a future filled with possibility.

CHAPTER TWENTY-NINE

The Challenge Ahead

The morning sun filtered through the trees, casting a golden hue over the campsite. Kartik, Arushi, Aniket, and Meera sat around the breakfast table, enjoying a simple meal of sandwiches and fresh fruit. The air was filled with laughter as they reminisced about the previous day's adventures.

Aniket: "Can you believe Meera almost slipped off that rock by the waterfall? I thought we were going to lose her to the river!"

Meera: "Oh please, I was perfectly fine! I was just testing my balancing skills. Besides, I have to keep you guys entertained somehow!"

Kartik smiled, his heart swelling with gratitude for this friendship. But then, he turned serious.

Kartik: "Guys, I've been thinking... We've had so much fun here, but we can't forget about our responsibilities back home."

Arushi: "I know what you mean. I've been trying to balance my work and this trip. It's challenging but worth it."

Aniket nodded, his expression thoughtful.

Aniket: "True. But let's make a pact: when we get back, we each set a goal for ourselves. Something that pushes us."

Meera: "I love that idea! What kind of goals are we talking about?"

Kartik took a deep breath, feeling a surge of confidence.

Kartik: "For me, it's finishing the first draft of my book. I want to write at least a few pages every day."

Arushi: "That's a great goal, Kartik. And you know we'll be here to support you. I want to focus on my career development and maybe take on more leadership responsibilities at work."

Aniket: "I'm in! I want to train for a half marathon. I've been saying I would do it for ages, and it's time to actually start."

Meera: "And I want to explore more creative hobbies. Maybe start painting or something artsy. I've always wanted to give it a shot."

They all agreed, and the energy shifted as they began discussing how they would hold each other accountable.

Kartik: "Let's set a weekly check-in. We can motivate each other and share our progress."

Aniket: "Definitely! We can meet at the café every Sunday. What do you think?"

Meera: "Perfect! It'll be our little support group. I love it!"

As they finished their breakfast, a sense of determination filled the air. They packed their bags, ready to head back to the city, but not before one last adventure in the woods.

Kartik: "Before we leave, how about we go for a short hike? Just a quick one to soak in the nature one last time."

Arushi: "I'm in! Let's do it!"

The four friends set out on a trail that led deeper into the woods, the sounds of nature enveloping them. The path was narrow, and the trees loomed tall, creating a canopy of green overhead. They walked in pairs, with Kartik and Arushi in the front, and Aniket and Meera chatting behind them.

Kartik glanced over at Arushi, her hair gently swaying in the breeze.

Kartik: "You know, I've always admired how confident you are. It's inspiring."

Arushi: "Thanks, Kartik. I guess it comes from believing in myself. But I see that same strength in you. You just need to let it shine."

He nodded, contemplating her words. They reached a clearing, and the view took their breath away—a vast valley stretching out below them. The sky was painted in shades of blue and orange, a perfect backdrop for a moment of reflection.

Kartik: "This is incredible. It feels like we're on top of the world."

Arushi: "It really does. I'm glad we took this trip. It's given me clarity."

Meanwhile, Aniket and Meera caught up, enjoying the view from the edge of the clearing.

Aniket: "What do you think will happen when we get back? Things will be different, right?"

Meera: "Absolutely! We've all grown so much during this trip. I think we'll approach challenges with a new mindset."

Aniket: "And we'll have each other's backs, no matter what. That's what makes it all worth it."

They joined Kartik and Arushi at the edge of the clearing, standing together, taking in the beauty around them.

Kartik: "No matter what challenges we face, I believe we'll overcome them together."

Arushi: "Exactly. This is just the beginning of our journey, and I can't wait to see what lies ahead for all of us."

As they made their way back to the campsite, a sense of excitement filled the air. They felt invigorated, ready to tackle their individual goals and support each other in the process.

Kartik: "Let's make a promise. No matter how busy life gets, we'll always prioritize our dreams and friendship."

They all nodded in agreement, a smile spreading across their faces as they solidified their commitment to each other.

Aniket: "Deal! To our dreams!"

Meera: "And to our friendship!"

Arushi: "To us!"

CHAPTER THIRTY

Turning Points

The sun dipped low on the horizon as the friends left the restaurant, the evening air crisp and refreshing. With a sense of purpose, they strolled through the bustling streets of the city, each lost in their thoughts about the future.

Kartik: "What a great night! I feel like we really solidified our plans."

Aniket: "Definitely! But now it's time to put those plans into action. I'm excited to start my training tomorrow."

Meera: "Speaking of action, I should start brainstorming for my new art piece. Maybe I'll do a piece inspired by our trip?"

Arushi: "That's a great idea, Meera! Your paintings always capture emotion so well. You could channel the feelings from our adventure."

Kartik: "What about our favorite moments? Maybe we could all collaborate on something, like a blog post or a video montage."

As they walked, they reached a small park where a fountain sparkled under the streetlights. They decided to sit on a nearby bench. The atmosphere was tranquil, a stark contrast to the city's hustle and bustle.

Aniket: "You know, it's moments like these that remind me why we need to stay connected. Life gets busy, but it's the people around us that make it worthwhile."

Meera: "I agree! Let's make it a point to have regular catch-ups, even if it's just over coffee."

Kartik: "For sure! How about a monthly get-together? We can share updates on our goals and keep each other motivated."

Arushi: "I love that idea! We should also include some fun activities, like game nights or creative sessions."

Their laughter echoed in the quiet park, and Kartik felt a sense of warmth spread through him. He had always been the quiet observer, but now he felt more confident than ever.

Kartik: "I want to challenge myself to step out of my comfort zone. Maybe I'll do a reading at a local event."

Aniket: "That's awesome, Kartik! You've got the talent; now it's time to showcase it."

Meera: "And I'll help you prepare! I'd love to see you shine."

Arushi: "You've got this, Kartik! Just remember, we'll be there cheering you on."

As the conversation flowed, they delved deeper into their personal aspirations. Aniket opened up about his dreams of participating in a marathon.

Aniket: "I've always wanted to challenge myself physically. Running that marathon will be a huge accomplishment for me."

Meera: "You can totally do it! Just keep pushing yourself, and you'll cross that finish line."

Arushi: "We should come to support you! We'll make posters and cheer for you."

Kartik: "I'll even run alongside you for part of it if you want some company."

Aniket grinned, feeling the encouragement from his friends. The shared dreams were a reminder of their strength as a group.

Aniket: "You guys are the best! I can't wait to make all these plans a reality."

The night began to deepen, and the stars sparkled overhead. Arushi turned her gaze to the sky, her heart filled with possibilities.

Arushi: "I've been thinking about my career path. I want to take more initiative and perhaps even explore leadership roles."

Kartik: "You'd be a fantastic leader, Arushi. You have the vision and drive to inspire others."

Meera: "And the team would be lucky to have you guiding them. Just don't hesitate to take that step!"

Inspired by the conversations, they began discussing ways to support each other in their pursuits, the excitement palpable. Each friend felt invigorated by the possibilities ahead.

Kartik: "We should create a vision board together. It could help us visualize our goals and keep us motivated."

Aniket: "Yes! Let's meet next weekend for a vision board party. We can share our dreams and get creative."

Meera: "I'll bring my art supplies! It'll be a fun and productive day."

Arushi: "I'll prepare snacks. This is going to be so much fun!"

As they made their plans, a sense of unity enveloped them. Each friend felt more connected than ever, realizing how vital their relationships were to their individual journeys. They shared their dreams, fears, and aspirations, forging an unbreakable bond.

Kartik: "I'm so grateful for all of you. This journey is going to be incredible."

Aniket: "And it's just the beginning! Together, we can achieve anything."

Meera: "Absolutely! Let's lift each other up and make our dreams come true."

Arushi: "Here's to our future! May it be filled with laughter, growth, and success."

With that, they sat in comfortable silence, absorbing the moment. The city lights twinkled around them, and for the first time in a long time, each of them felt hopeful about what lay ahead. They were ready to embrace the challenges and adventures that awaited, knowing they had each other to lean on.

The night was still young, but their hearts were already full of dreams, aspirations, and a promise to support one another every step of the way.

CHAPTER THIRTY-ONE

Vision in Motion

The following weekend arrived with a bright sun and clear skies, setting the perfect backdrop for their vision board party. Kartik's apartment buzzed with excitement as Meera and Aniket arrived, carrying bags filled with art supplies and snacks. Arushi was already there, arranging the living room into a cozy creative space.

Arushi: "Welcome, everyone! I'm so glad you could make it. I set up the table for our vision boards over here."

Meera: "I brought magazines, colored markers, and glue sticks! We're going to make these boards pop!"

Aniket: "I can't wait! This is going to be so much fun. Who knew planning our futures could be this exciting?"

As they settled into their creative space, they discussed their dreams and goals, sharing inspirations and ideas.

Kartik: "So, how should we start? Should we each share our goals first?"

Arushi: "Absolutely! Let's share what we hope to achieve, and then we can find images and quotes that resonate with our visions."

Kartik took a deep breath, feeling a mix of nervousness and excitement. He admired his friends' confidence and knew this was his chance to open up.

Kartik: "Okay, I'll go first. I want to publish my book this year. I've been working on it for a while, and I want it to be out in the world, inspiring others."

Meera: "That's amazing, Kartik! Your story deserves to be told. I'll find some quotes and images that represent your journey."

Encouraged by his friends' enthusiasm, Kartik felt a surge of motivation. They took turns sharing their aspirations, creating an atmosphere filled with positivity and encouragement.

Aniket: "I want to run that marathon and improve my fitness. I've never pushed myself physically like this before, but I believe I can do it."

Arushi: "You're going to crush it! Let's find some powerful images of athletes and quotes about perseverance."

Meera: "And I want to have my art displayed in a gallery! That's my big dream. I'll find inspiration from other artists who have made it big."

As they continued to share their dreams, the energy in the room intensified. It became clear that this gathering was more than just a crafting session; it was a celebration of their collective ambitions.

Arushi: "I want to take on more leadership roles in my career. I've been hesitant, but I know I can make a difference."

Kartik: "You'll be a fantastic leader, Arushi. Your vision and empathy will inspire so many."

Once everyone had shared their dreams, they dove into their projects, cutting out images and quotes that resonated with their goals. Laughter and creativity filled the room as they encouraged one another, offering constructive feedback and support.

Meera: "Look at this quote! 'Believe you can, and you're halfway there.' This perfectly represents all of us!"

Aniket: "That's going on my board for sure. It's a great reminder to keep pushing forward."

Kartik: "I found this image of a person standing at the edge of a cliff, looking out at a beautiful horizon. It symbolizes taking that leap into the unknown with confidence."

Arushi: "That's perfect! It captures the essence of your journey so well."

As the afternoon turned into evening, their vision boards began to take shape, each reflecting their unique aspirations and personalities. The excitement in the air was palpable, and each of them felt a renewed sense of purpose.

Meera: "I can't believe how much I've already created! This is turning out to be one of my favorite days."

Aniket: "And we're not done yet! Let's set a deadline for our goals. How about we all check in with each other in three months to see our progress?"

Kartik: "I love that idea! It'll keep us accountable and motivated."

Arushi: "Agreed! We can have a follow-up meeting to share what we've accomplished and encourage each other."

As they wrapped up their creative session, Kartik felt a warmth in his heart. He realized how lucky he was to have friends who supported him unconditionally. The vision boards were not just pieces of art; they represented their commitment to each other's dreams.

Kartik: "Thank you, everyone, for making this such a special day. I'm grateful to have you all in my life."

Meera: "We're all in this together, Kartik. Let's keep lifting each other up."

Aniket: "Here's to our dreams becoming reality!"

Arushi: "To friendship, dreams, and the adventures ahead!"

With their vision boards complete, they gathered for a group photo, capturing the moment. Each friend held up their boards proudly, their faces beaming with hope and determination. This day marked the beginning of a new chapter in their lives—a chapter where they would chase their dreams together, supporting one another every step of the way.

As they packed up, the laughter and conversations continued, and Kartik felt lighter, ready to embrace the challenges ahead. The journey ahead may be uncertain, but with his friends by his side, he knew they could overcome anything.

CHAPTER THIRTY-TWO

Uncharted Waters

Weeks passed since the vision board party, and Kartik could feel the excitement of his dreams coming to life. With each passing day, he worked diligently on his book, inspired by the support of Arushi, Meera, and Aniket. However, a new challenge loomed ahead. The company announced a major project that required all hands on deck, leading to late nights and increased pressure.

One evening, while Kartik was burning the midnight oil at his desk, he received a message from Arushi.

Arushi: "Hey, just checking in! How's the writing going? ?"

Kartik paused, smiling at the message, feeling a wave of encouragement wash over him.

Kartik: "It's going well! I'm almost at the climax of the story. But the new project has made it a bit challenging to focus."

Arushi: "I get it! We've all been swamped lately. Just remember to take breaks. You're doing amazing work!"

Kartik felt a warmth in his chest, grateful for her unwavering support. It was during these late nights that he realized how much Arushi meant to him. The realization hit him like a wave; he had fallen for her deeper than he had acknowledged.

The next day, as the team gathered for a meeting to discuss the new project, Kartik noticed how stress levels were rising. Everyone seemed to be feeling the pressure.

Aniket: "Okay, team, let's tackle this project head-on. I know it's going to be tough, but we've done bigger things before."

Meera: "Right! Let's keep the energy high. We can do this together!"

Kartik could see the determination in their faces, and he felt a surge of motivation to contribute even more. They split into smaller groups, tackling different aspects of the project, but Kartik couldn't shake the feeling of wanting to talk to Arushi about his feelings. The chaos of the project made him realize he couldn't wait any longer.*

One evening, as they wrapped up a long day of meetings, Kartik found Arushi packing her things. He took a deep breath and approached her.

Kartik: "Hey, Arushi, do you have a moment?"

Arushi looked up, a smile breaking through the exhaustion on her face.

Arushi: "Of course! What's up?"

Kartik hesitated for a moment, searching for the right words. His heart raced as he prepared to reveal his feelings.

Kartik: "I wanted to talk to you about something important. I've been meaning to say it for a while, and with everything going on, I think I need to share it now."

Arushi's eyes softened, and she nodded encouragingly.

Arushi: "I'm all ears."

Kartik took a deep breath, steeling himself for what he was about to say.

Kartik: "I've realized that my feelings for you have grown. I admire your strength, your determination, and how you always push everyone to be better. I can't ignore it anymore—Arushi, I think I'm falling in love with you."

A silence enveloped them, and Kartik's heart raced. He could see surprise flicker in Arushi's eyes, quickly replaced by something deeper.

Arushi: "Kartik... I—"

Kartik, fearing he had misread the situation, rushed to fill the silence.

Kartik: "I know we've been friends, and I value that deeply, but I needed to be honest. I don't expect anything, but I had to let you know."

Arushi took a moment, her gaze piercing into Kartik's heart. A smile slowly spread across her face.

Arushi: "I'm so glad you said that. I've been feeling the same way but didn't know how to express it. It's been a whirlwind of emotions, especially with everything happening at work."

Kartik felt relief wash over him, and the weight he had carried for weeks lifted.

Kartik: "Really? You mean it?"

Arushi nodded, her eyes shining.

Arushi: "Yes! I've admired you for your kindness and depth. I just didn't want to complicate things, especially now."

As they stood there, everything around them faded. The noise of the office dimmed, and all that mattered was this moment. Kartik reached for her hand, a mixture of excitement and nervousness flooding through him.

Kartik: "So, what does this mean for us?"

Arushi squeezed his hand, her voice firm yet gentle.

Arushi: "It means we take it one step at a time. I want to explore this with you, Kartik. Together."

Kartik couldn't help but grin, the connection they shared deepening with every word. They spent the next hour talking, laughing, and sharing their hopes for the future. For the first time in weeks, Kartik felt a sense of peace amidst the chaos of the project.

Days turned into weeks, and their relationship blossomed amidst the pressures of work. Kartik found himself more inspired than ever, writing diligently and pouring his heart into his book. The team rallied together, facing the project's challenges with renewed determination, fueled by Kartik and Arushi's budding relationship.

One Friday evening, they decided to celebrate the completion of a significant milestone in their project. Aniket and Meera organized a small get-together at a local café, and the atmosphere was filled with laughter and joy.

Aniket: "Here's to all the hard work and the milestones we've achieved together! And to new beginnings!"

Meera: "And to love! I can't believe Kartik finally confessed. You guys are adorable!"

Kartik and Arushi exchanged shy glances, their hands subtly intertwined under the table. The warmth of their connection radiated through the group, and everyone could feel the change in their dynamic.*

Meera: "So, what's next for the lovebirds?"

Arushi, with a teasing smile, turned to Kartik.

Arushi: "Well, we're going to make time for our dreams while supporting each other, right?"

Kartik: "Absolutely. We have our vision boards to keep us on track!"

The evening continued with playful banter and heartfelt toasts. Kartik felt an overwhelming sense of gratitude for the friendships that had blossomed alongside his growing love for Arushi.

As they left the café, Kartik and Arushi lingered behind, sharing quiet laughter. The night was cool, and the stars twinkled above them like the dreams they had laid out on their vision boards.

Arushi: "I'm really glad you took that leap, Kartik. You've opened a whole new chapter in my life."

Kartik: "I couldn't have done it without your encouragement. You inspire me every day."

Arushi: "And you remind me to embrace my true self. I'm excited to see where this journey takes us."

Kartik looked at her, the stars reflecting in her eyes, and felt a sense of certainty he had never experienced before. In this moment, he knew they were destined to explore uncharted waters together, ready to embrace whatever challenges lay ahead.*

As they walked side by side, Kartik felt the pulse of possibility in the air, a promise of love intertwined with the pursuit of their dreams. Together, they were ready to conquer the world.

CHAPTER THIRTY-THREE

Navigating New Challenges

As spring blossomed, bringing warmth and vitality to their lives, Kartik and Arushi settled into a comfortable rhythm in both their personal and professional lives. However, with success often came unexpected challenges. The project was nearing its final phases, and with it came an increased workload, deadlines, and expectations. Despite the stress, Kartik felt more motivated than ever, driven by the support he received from Arushi and his friends.

One afternoon, as they took a break from work, Aniket approached Kartik, a concerned look on his face.

Aniket: "Hey, Kartik. Can we talk for a minute?"

Kartik nodded, sensing the seriousness in Aniket's tone.

Kartik: "Sure, what's up?"

Aniket led Kartik to a quieter corner of the office, away from the bustling energy of their teammates.

Aniket: "I've noticed you've been pushing yourself pretty hard lately. Are you okay?"

Kartik let out a sigh, running a hand through his hair.

Kartik: "Yeah, I'm fine. Just trying to balance everything. The project is a lot, but I want to finish strong."

Aniket: "I get that, but don't forget to take care of yourself. You're doing great work, but burnout isn't worth it."

Kartik appreciated Aniket's concern but brushed it off.

Kartik: "Thanks, Aniket, but I promise I'm managing. Arushi and I are in this together, and it keeps me motivated."

Aniket smiled, visibly relieved to see Kartik in good spirits.

Aniket: "Alright, just checking in. Remember, we're all here to help each other out."

Kartik nodded, grateful for his friend's support. As he returned to his desk, he couldn't shake the feeling of weight on his shoulders. The pressure was building, and he knew he needed to find a way to balance it all without losing sight of what truly mattered.*

That evening, after a long day of meetings, Kartik and Arushi met at their favorite café to unwind. The ambiance was cozy, filled with the chatter of patrons and the aroma of freshly brewed coffee. They settled into a corner table, and Arushi looked at Kartik, concern etched on her face.

Arushi: "Kartik, you've been working nonstop. Are you sure you're okay?"

Kartik forced a smile, though he felt the fatigue creeping in.

Kartik: "I'm good, just a bit overwhelmed with everything going on. But I'll manage."

Arushi leaned in closer, her gaze intense.

Arushi: "You don't have to carry it all by yourself. Remember, I'm here for you. Let's tackle things together."

Kartik felt a warmth in his chest, grateful for her support.

Kartik: "I know, and I appreciate it. I guess I just want to prove myself, especially now that we're together."

Arushi reached across the table, taking his hand in hers.

Arushi: "You already have. You don't need to prove anything to anyone, least of all to me. Just be yourself."

Kartik squeezed her hand, feeling a sense of reassurance wash over him.

Kartik: "Thanks, Arushi. I needed that reminder."

As they chatted about their dreams and aspirations, the conversation shifted to their vision boards.

Arushi: "I've been thinking about mine. I want to incorporate more travel this year. Maybe we could plan a trip together?"

Kartik's eyes lit up at the idea. The thought of exploring new places with Arushi filled him with excitement.

Kartik: "That sounds amazing! I'd love to travel with you. Any particular destinations in mind?"

Arushi grinned, her enthusiasm infectious.

Arushi: "I've always wanted to visit the mountains. There's something about being surrounded by nature that feels so refreshing."

Kartik nodded, already envisioning the serene landscapes they could explore together.

Kartik: "Mountains it is! Let's make it happen. We could use a break from all this work."

Arushi: "Absolutely! We'll recharge our batteries and come back even stronger."

As they left the café, Kartik felt invigorated by their conversation and the prospect of an adventure with Arushi. However, the pressure from work continued to loom over him. The project deadlines were closing in, and the stress started to manifest physically. He found himself waking up in the middle of the night, unable to shake off the worries that danced in his mind.

One evening, while reviewing documents at home, Kartik received a call from Meera.

Meera: "Hey, Kartik! I wanted to check in and see how you're doing. You've been awfully quiet lately."

Kartik leaned back in his chair, grateful for her call.

Kartik: "Hey, Meera! I'm okay, just a bit swamped with the project. It's been intense."

Meera's voice turned serious.

Meera: "Kartik, don't forget to take breaks. You need to give yourself some space to breathe. How's Arushi handling it all?"

Kartik: "She's great! She's been supportive, but I feel like I need to step up and prove my worth."

Meera paused for a moment, considering his words.

Meera: "You don't need to prove anything to anyone. Just be the amazing person you are. It's okay to lean on your friends for support."

Kartik appreciated her words but felt a nagging pressure to succeed. They continued to chat, and Meera's encouragement reminded him that he wasn't alone.*

As the project neared completion, Kartik decided to take a step back and evaluate what truly mattered. He sat down with Arushi one evening after work, wanting to share his thoughts.

Kartik: "Arushi, can we talk about something?"

Arushi looked up from her laptop, sensing the seriousness in his tone.

Arushi: "Of course! What's on your mind?"

Kartik took a deep breath, gathering his thoughts.

Kartik: "I've been feeling the pressure lately, and it's starting to take a toll on me. I don't want to lose sight of what we have because of work."

Arushi leaned in, concern filling her eyes.

Arushi: "Kartik, I get it. The project has been tough, but we can find a balance. You don't have to sacrifice your well-being for it."

Kartik nodded, feeling the weight of her words.

Kartik: "You're right. I want to make sure we're both happy, not just focused on work. I don't want to overlook our dreams."

Arushi smiled, her hand gently touching his.

Arushi: "We'll figure it out together. Let's make time for our dreams and for each other. It's essential to have both."

Kartik felt a renewed sense of determination as they discussed ways to manage their work and personal lives. They made a plan to prioritize self-care, set boundaries, and ensure that they never lost sight of their goals as a couple.*

With newfound clarity, Kartik approached the final phase of the project with a fresh mindset. He delegated tasks more effectively, leaned on his teammates for support, and made sure to take breaks. The pressure eased, and he felt invigorated by the prospect of finishing strong.

As the project reached its final deadline, Kartik and Arushi celebrated their achievements together, grateful for the support they provided one another. The experience not only strengthened their relationship but also reminded them of the importance of navigating challenges as a team.

One afternoon, after completing a critical presentation, the team gathered to celebrate their success. Aniket raised his glass, a wide grin on his face.

Aniket: "To teamwork and success! We did it, everyone! This project wouldn't have been possible without each of you!"

Meera: "And let's not forget to celebrate Kartik and Arushi! Their collaboration was key!"

Kartik and Arushi exchanged shy smiles, feeling a rush of pride.

Kartik: "Thanks, everyone! This is a team effort, and I couldn't have done it without all of you."

Arushi: "Here's to our hard work paying off and to new adventures ahead!"

As the evening drew to a close, Kartik felt a sense of accomplishment and joy. He knew that while challenges would continue to arise, he and Arushi had the strength and support of their friends to navigate through them. Their love had become a powerful force, propelling them toward their dreams while grounding them in reality.

With renewed focus, Kartik set his sights on completing his book, ready to embrace the journey ahead. Together with Arushi, they were ready to face whatever challenges came their way, side by side.

CHAPTER THIRTY-FOUR

Beyond the Horizon

As summer approached, bringing longer days and a vibrant energy to their lives, Kartik and Arushi found themselves in a period of reflection and excitement. The successful completion of their project had sparked a newfound confidence in Kartik, igniting his creative spirit. With a clear mind, he turned his focus to finishing his book, eager to share their journey and the lessons they had learned along the way.

One evening, as they sat together in their living room, Kartik was typing furiously on his laptop, and Arushi was curled up on the couch with a book. She glanced up, noticing Kartik's intensity.

Arushi: "Hey, what's got you so focused? You look like you're on a mission."

Kartik paused, looking up with a smile.

Kartik: "I am! I'm finally finishing the chapter about our project and how it brought us closer together. It feels like a pivotal moment in both our lives."

Arushi set her book aside, intrigued.

Arushi: "That sounds great! I'd love to hear what you've written so far."

Kartik turned his laptop toward her, scrolling to the relevant section. He read aloud, his voice filled with emotion.

Kartik: "I wrote about how the challenges we faced together taught us the importance of communication and support. It's not just about the work but about the bond we share that helps us grow."

Arushi smiled, her heart swelling with pride.

Arushi: "That's beautiful, Kartik. It's so true. I think our experiences have made us stronger, both individually and as a couple."

Kartik looked at her, feeling a rush of gratitude.

Kartik: "I couldn't have done it without you. You inspire me every day to be better."

Arushi's cheeks flushed as she brushed her hair behind her ear.

Arushi: "You make me want to be better too. It's a mutual growth journey."

As they continued discussing the book, the conversation shifted to their upcoming trip to the mountains. The excitement of exploring together was palpable, and they made a list of things they wanted to do while they were away.

Kartik: "We should definitely go hiking! I've read about some incredible trails in the area."

Arushi: "Yes! And don't forget to pack our camera. I want to capture every moment with you."

Kartik grinned, his enthusiasm matching hers.

Kartik: "Absolutely! Let's make this a trip to remember."

Days turned into weeks, and the anticipation of their mountain getaway filled them with joy. They spent evenings preparing, packing their bags, and planning their itinerary. On the day of their departure, the excitement was electric as they loaded the car with their essentials. Aniket and Meera had decided to join them, adding to the adventure.

Meera: "I can't believe we're finally doing this! A weekend in the mountains is exactly what we need."

Aniket: "And I've packed all the snacks! We won't go hungry, that's for sure!"

Kartik: "Just make sure we leave some room for our hiking gear!"

They all laughed as they piled into the car, their spirits high. The road trip was filled with music, laughter, and chatter, each mile drawing them closer to their destination. As they climbed higher into the mountains, the air grew crisper, and the scenery transformed into a breathtaking panorama of lush greenery and towering peaks.*

When they finally arrived at their cabin, they were awestruck by the beauty that surrounded them. The sun dipped low in the sky, casting a golden hue over the landscape. Arushi stepped out of the car, inhaling the fresh mountain air, feeling a wave of tranquility wash over her.

Arushi: "Wow, this place is incredible! Just look at the view!"

Kartik took her hand, pulling her closer as they both admired the scenery.

Kartik: "This is just the beginning. We have so much to explore!"

After settling in, they decided to go for a short hike before dinner. The trail was well-marked, winding through the trees, and filled with the sounds of chirping birds and rustling leaves. As they walked, Kartik and Arushi fell into an easy conversation, sharing stories and laughter, while Aniket and Meera playfully challenged each other to see who could find the best hiking spot.

Aniket: "Bet I can find the highest rock to sit on!"

Meera: "Oh please, it's not about the height; it's about the view!"

Kartik and Arushi exchanged amused glances, reveling in the lighthearted banter of their friends. They soon reached a clearing that overlooked a stunning valley, where the sunset painted the sky in hues of orange, pink, and purple.*

Kartik: "This is perfect! Let's take a picture!"

They all gathered together, smiling as the camera clicked, capturing the essence of the moment. The beauty of nature around them and the warmth of friendship filled their hearts.*

That night, as they gathered around the fireplace in the cabin, they shared stories, laughter, and a few heartfelt moments. The flickering flames cast a warm glow, and Kartik felt grateful for this time together.

Meera: "I love how peaceful it is out here. It's like we've stepped into a different world."

Arushi: "Exactly! It reminds me of why we needed this break in the first place. Just to breathe."

Kartik: "And to reconnect with each other. We're so caught up in our daily lives that we forget to enjoy the little moments."

Aniket raised his glass, ready for a toast.

Aniket: "To friendship, adventure, and the beauty of living in the moment!"

They clinked their glasses together, a sense of camaraderie and love enveloping them. Kartik felt a profound sense of belonging, knowing they were creating memories that would last a lifetime.*

As the night wore on, the conversation turned more introspective. They each took turns sharing their hopes and dreams for the future.

Arushi: "I want to travel the world, experience new cultures, and grow both personally and professionally. I believe there's so much out there waiting for us."

Kartik: "And I want to share my stories with others, to inspire them through my writing. I want my book to reach people and make a difference."

Meera: "I want to open my own design studio one day. I've been working on my portfolio, and I feel like it's finally coming together."

Aniket: "For me, it's about making a positive impact in my community. I want to help others find their passion and guide them toward their goals."

The night grew late, and one by one, they headed off to bed, leaving Kartik and Arushi sitting by the fire, the embers glowing softly. Kartik looked at Arushi, his heart full.

Kartik: "I'm so glad we're here together. These moments make everything worthwhile."

Arushi smiled, her eyes sparkling in the firelight.

Arushi: "Me too, Kartik. This is just the beginning of many adventures to come."

As they sat in comfortable silence, they both knew that the journey ahead would be filled with challenges, but with love and friendship as their foundation, they could face anything together. The horizon was wide open, and they were ready to embrace it.*

CHAPTER THIRTY-FIVE

Embracing the Unknown

The next day dawned bright and clear, with the sun shining through the trees, casting dappled shadows on the ground. The air was fresh, and the aroma of pine filled their senses as Kartik, Arushi, Aniket, and Meera gathered for breakfast. Excitement buzzed among them as they sipped their coffee and planned the day's adventures.

Kartik: "So, what's the plan for today? I heard there's a stunning waterfall hike not too far from here."

Meera: "I'm in! I love waterfalls. They're so peaceful and beautiful."

Aniket: "Sounds good to me! I'll pack the snacks. Can't hike on an empty stomach!"

Arushi: "I'll grab the camera! We need to capture every moment."

After breakfast, they geared up for the hike, ensuring they had everything they needed—water bottles, snacks, and of course, their cameras. The group set off down the trail, the anticipation building with every step. As they walked, they laughed, told stories, and took turns sharing their thoughts about the beautiful surroundings.

Arushi: "Look at those wildflowers! They're so vibrant. Nature is truly an artist."

Kartik paused to admire the flowers, snapping a quick photo.

Kartik: "They really are stunning. Just like you."

Arushi blushed, a smile spreading across her face.

Arushi: "You always know how to make me feel special, Kartik."

Aniket pretended to gag, lightening the mood.

Aniket: "Oh, come on! Save the lovey-dovey stuff for later. We've got a waterfall to chase!"

Meera laughed, nudging Aniket playfully.

Meera: "Let them have their moment! Besides, love is what makes adventures even more exciting!"

The trail began to steepen as they approached the waterfall, and the sound of rushing water grew louder. The anticipation was palpable, and Kartik felt a rush of adrenaline. With each step, he could almost envision the breathtaking sight awaiting them. Finally, they rounded a bend, and the waterfall came into view. It was magnificent—a cascade of crystal-clear water tumbling over smooth rocks, creating a sparkling pool below.

Arushi: "Wow! It's even more beautiful than I imagined!"

Kartik nodded, unable to tear his eyes away from the sight. They all stood in awe, the roar of the water filling the air, drowning out their voices. After a moment, Aniket broke the silence.*

Aniket: "Alright, who's the first brave soul to go for a swim?"

Meera grinned mischievously.

Meera: "I'll do it if you do it!"

Kartik: "You guys are crazy! It's freezing!"

Arushi looked at Kartik, her eyes sparkling with mischief.

Arushi: "Come on, Kartik! It'll be fun! Besides, it'll make for a great story!"

Kartik hesitated, but the thrill of the moment was hard to resist. With a deep breath, he decided to join in. The four of them raced to the edge of the water, and with a loud splash, they jumped in together. Laughter filled the air as they surfaced, shivering but exhilarated.*

Kartik: "Okay, that was freezing but totally worth it!"

Meera: "See? You survived! Now let's take some pictures!"

As they swam and splashed in the cool water, Kartik couldn't help but feel a sense of freedom. He was living in the moment, embracing the unknown, and surrounded by people who brought joy and laughter into his life. After a while, they all climbed out, shivering but happy. They found a sunny spot on the rocks to dry off and enjoy their snacks.

Aniket: "I can't believe we actually jumped in! That was awesome!"

Meera: "Next time, let's bring towels! I didn't expect to get this wet."

Kartik looked at Arushi, a grin spreading across his face.

Kartik: "Best decision ever?"

Arushi laughed, her eyes sparkling in the sunlight.

Arushi: "Definitely! This day just keeps getting better."

After their impromptu swim, they decided to explore the area around the waterfall. They wandered along the rocky banks, finding small caves and hidden spots. Kartik felt a surge of inspiration as he snapped photos, capturing the beauty of the moment and the joy of their friendship.

Kartik: "This place is perfect for my book! The waterfall symbolizes the flow of life—sometimes unpredictable, but beautiful in its own way."

Arushi: "That's a lovely analogy. It really fits our journey, doesn't it? We've faced challenges, but we've come out stronger."

Aniket and Meera exchanged knowing glances, recognizing the depth of their conversation.

Aniket: "You two are getting all philosophical on us. Let's take some more pictures instead!"

Meera: "Yes! Let's create memories we can look back on!"

They gathered for more photos, striking silly poses and capturing candid moments that spoke of their friendship and connection. After a few hours of exploration, they decided it was time to head back to the cabin. As they walked, they reflected on the day's adventures.

Arushi: "I'll never forget this day. It felt like we were part of something magical."

Kartik: "Agreed. I'm so glad we did this together. Moments like these remind me why I love writing. It's about preserving the magic."

When they returned to the cabin, they gathered around the fireplace once again, exhausted but exhilarated. As they shared stories from their hike and the hilarity of their swim, Kartik felt a sense of contentment wash over him.

Meera: "I can't believe how much fun we had! We should do this more often."

Aniket: "Definitely! Next time, we should bring even more people and make it a big group adventure."

Kartik smiled, looking at Arushi.*

Kartik: "Count me in! I love how our friendships grow stronger with each adventure."

Arushi reached over, squeezing his hand.

Arushi: "And I love how we're all in this together. This is just the beginning of many more adventures to come."

As the fire crackled and the stars twinkled outside, they settled in for the night, their hearts full of gratitude and anticipation for what lay ahead. Kartik felt a renewed sense of purpose, ready to embrace whatever challenges and joys awaited him, alongside Arushi and their friends. The journey of life, much like their hike, was filled with unexpected turns, but with love and friendship, they could navigate anything together.

CHAPTER THIRTY-SIX

A Heartfelt Confession

The sun rose the next morning, casting a warm golden hue over the forest. Kartik woke up early, the tranquility of nature surrounding him. He stepped outside the cabin, taking a deep breath of the crisp morning air. The events of the previous day replayed in his mind—laughter, friendship, and the thrill of adventure. However, there was also a weight on his heart, a feeling he could no longer ignore. He wanted to tell Arushi how he truly felt.

As he stood on the porch, lost in thought, Aniket came out, rubbing his eyes.

Aniket: "You're up early! Can't sleep?"

Kartik turned, forcing a smile.

Kartik: "Just enjoying the quiet. It's peaceful out here."

Aniket leaned against the railing, sensing something deeper beneath Kartik's calm facade.

Aniket: "You look like you're contemplating the meaning of life. What's going on?"

Kartik sighed, knowing he couldn't hide it any longer.

Kartik: "I've been thinking about Arushi. I need to tell her how I feel, but I'm not sure how she'll react."

Aniket's expression shifted from sleepy to serious.

Aniket: "Dude, you can't keep it bottled up. You've got to be honest with her. She deserves to know."

Kartik nodded, his heart racing at the thought of confessing his feelings.

Kartik: "What if she doesn't feel the same way? I don't want to ruin our friendship."

Aniket shrugged.

Aniket: "That's a risk you have to take. But think about it: what if she does feel the same way? You'll never know unless you try."

Kartik took a deep breath, weighing Aniket's words. With newfound determination, he decided that today would be the day he expressed his feelings to Arushi. As the group gathered for breakfast, the atmosphere was light and cheerful, filled with teasing and laughter. Kartik's heart raced as he caught Arushi's eye. He felt a mixture of excitement and fear as the meal progressed.

Meera: "So, what's the plan for today? More adventures?"

Arushi looked around, her eyes sparkling with enthusiasm.

Arushi: "I think we should explore that hiking trail we saw yesterday! It looked amazing!"

Aniket: "Count me in! I'll be the navigator."

Kartik's heart pounded in his chest as he prepared to speak up. He cleared his throat, gathering his courage.

Kartik: "Um, guys, can we take a little detour first? I... I need to talk to Arushi for a moment."

The group exchanged curious glances as Kartik gestured for Arushi to follow him. Aniket gave a supportive nod, and Meera smiled encouragingly. Kartik led Arushi a short distance away, where they could have some privacy among the trees. The atmosphere shifted from playful to serious as Kartik felt the weight of his confession pressing on him.*

Arushi: "What's on your mind, Kartik?"

Kartik hesitated, the words lodged in his throat. But he couldn't back down now. He looked deep into Arushi's eyes, gathering every ounce of courage.

Kartik: "Arushi, I've been thinking a lot about us. About what we have. You mean a lot to me, and I can't keep pretending that it's just friendship."

Arushi's expression shifted, surprise flickering in her eyes.

Arushi: "Kartik, I..."

Kartik continued, his voice steady but vulnerable.

Kartik: "I care about you more than just as a friend. I admire your strength, your kindness, and how you see the world. You make me want to be better. I just—"

Before he could finish, Arushi stepped closer, her eyes searching his.

Arushi: "Kartik, I never knew you felt this way."

Kartik took a deep breath, sensing the intensity of the moment.

Kartik: "I'm ordinary by looks, but extraordinary by heart. I want to know if you feel the same way."

Silence enveloped them, the air thick with unspoken emotions. Arushi looked at him, her expression softening. She took a moment to collect her thoughts before responding.*

Arushi: "Kartik, I've always appreciated you for who you are. I thought I was just being silly, but I think I've felt something deeper too. You bring so much joy into my life, and I don't want to lose that."

Kartik's heart raced, hope igniting within him.

Kartik: "So, what do you think? Could we explore this... together?"

Arushi smiled, a mixture of relief and excitement washing over her.

Arushi: "I'd like that. I really would."

As they stood there, surrounded by nature, a wave of warmth washed over them. Kartik took a step closer, feeling a sense of relief and happiness enveloping them both.

Kartik: "I've been waiting for the right moment to say this. Thank you for being you, Arushi. You make my life so much brighter."

Arushi beamed, her eyes sparkling with emotion.

Arushi: "And thank you for being brave enough to share your feelings. This is just the beginning, isn't it?"

Kartik nodded, his heart filled with hope and excitement.

Kartik: "Yes, it is."

They returned to their friends, their hearts lighter, and an unspoken bond growing between them. The day ahead felt full of promise as they embarked on their next adventure—together

CHAPTER THIRTY-SEVEN

A Day of Discovery

The morning sun shone brightly as the group set off on their hiking adventure. Kartik walked beside Arushi, their hands brushing occasionally, sending sparks of electricity through them. Aniket and Meera led the way, their laughter echoing through the trees as they enthusiastically planned their route.

Aniket: "I hope everyone is ready for a challenge! This trail is supposed to have some steep climbs, but the view at the top is worth it!"

Meera: "I brought some snacks for us to enjoy at the summit! Fuel for the climb!"

Kartik chuckled as he looked at Arushi, who was animatedly discussing the plans with Meera. The camaraderie between them felt warm and inviting. He turned to Arushi, a smile spreading across his face.

Kartik: "You're excited, huh? I can see it in your eyes."

Arushi paused, her expression shifting to one of pure joy.

Arushi: "I love the outdoors! Being out here makes me feel alive. Plus, sharing it with friends makes it even better!"

Kartik felt his heart swell at her enthusiasm. He wanted to create more memories like this—memories filled with laughter, adventure, and the growing connection between them. As they hiked, the path wound through dense trees and colorful wildflowers, each step bringing them closer together.*

After a while, they reached a clearing, a small plateau that offered a breathtaking view of the valley below. The sight was awe-inspiring, with rolling hills and vibrant greenery stretching as far as the eye could see. They all stood there in silence for a moment, soaking in the beauty.

Meera: "This is incredible! Look at that view! It feels like we're on top of the world!"

Aniket: "Perfect spot for a snack break, right?"

They settled down on the grass, unpacking their snacks and sharing stories about their childhood adventures. Laughter echoed as they recalled silly moments, each tale deepening their bond. Kartik and Arushi exchanged glances filled with unspoken understanding. The air was light, and the world outside this moment seemed to fade away.*

Kartik: "You know, I always wanted to explore the outdoors more, but I never found the right company until now."

Arushi smiled, her eyes sparkling in the sunlight.

Arushi: "I'm glad we're here together. It makes everything more special. I can't wait for our next adventure!"

Kartik nodded, feeling a warmth spreading through him. He leaned in closer, a playful glint in his eyes.

Kartik: "So, what's next on our adventure list? I hope it's something equally epic!"

Meera, overhearing their conversation, jumped in excitedly.

Meera: "How about a camping trip? Just the four of us under the stars, sharing stories by the campfire!"

Aniket's face lit up at the idea.

Aniket: "That sounds amazing! Count me in! I'll handle the firewood and cooking."

Arushi grinned, her eyes dancing with excitement.

Arushi: "And I can plan the snacks! We need the perfect s'mores for the campfire!"

Kartik felt a sense of belonging wash over him as they discussed their plans. This group of friends had become a significant part of his life, filling it with laughter and warmth. As they finished their snacks, Arushi turned to Kartik, her expression serious yet soft.

Arushi: "Hey, Kartik, can I ask you something?"

Kartik's heart raced slightly at the sudden change in her tone.

Kartik: "Of course! What's on your mind?"

Arushi hesitated, her brow furrowing slightly.

Arushi: "I've been thinking about... our friendship. I don't want things to change between us just because we're exploring something more."

Kartik reached out, placing his hand over hers, reassuring her.

Kartik: "I understand, Arushi. I don't want that either. Our friendship is important to me. Whatever happens, I want to make sure we're always there for each other."

She smiled, relief washing over her face.

Arushi: "Thank you, Kartik. That means a lot to me."

They shared a moment of silence, their hands lingering together, before Aniket interrupted with his usual exuberance.

Aniket: "Alright, enough of the mushy stuff! Let's conquer this trail!"

With that, they resumed their hike, the playful banter filling the air as they trekked onward. The path became steeper, and they found themselves encouraging one another, laughter ringing out as they stumbled over roots and rocks. Kartik felt a sense of exhilaration as they tackled each challenge together.*

After what felt like hours, they finally reached the summit. The view was even more breathtaking than before, the sky a brilliant blue, and the landscape sprawling endlessly. They all stood in awe, taking in the beauty of the world around them.

Meera: "This is it! This is what I came for!"

Aniket: "We did it, guys! Look at that view!"

Kartik glanced at Arushi, who was staring at the horizon, her expression thoughtful. He felt a surge of emotion, realizing how much he cherished this moment with her. He wanted to capture it forever, a memory of their adventure and the connection they were building.*

Kartik: "Arushi, can we take a picture together? To remember this moment?"

Her eyes brightened as she nodded.

Arushi: "Yes! Let's do it!"

They gathered together, arms around each other, laughter erupting as they struck silly poses. Aniket snapped several photos, capturing the joy and spontaneity of the moment. Afterward, they settled down on the grass, enjoying the gentle breeze and the tranquility of the summit.*

Arushi: "I can't believe we made it! This is the best day ever!"

Kartik: "It truly is. And I'm so glad to share it with you all."

Meera: "We should do this more often! Adventures like this are what life is all about!"

As they sat there, taking in the breathtaking view and the laughter shared among friends, Kartik couldn't help but feel grateful for this moment. It was more than just a day of hiking; it was a step toward something beautiful—a future filled with possibilities, laughter, and a bond that would only grow stronger.*

As the sun began to set, casting a golden hue over the landscape, Kartik felt a warmth spreading in his heart. He looked at Arushi, who was smiling brightly, her happiness contagious. He realized that this day, this moment, was just the beginning of their adventure together.

CHAPTER THIRTY-EIGHT

Under the Stars

As the sun dipped below the horizon, painting the sky with hues of orange and pink, the group started their descent from the summit. The evening air was cool and crisp, and the sounds of the forest surrounded them. Laughter filled the air as they reminisced about the day's adventures.

Aniket: "You know, we should definitely make this a tradition. Hiking, exploring new places, and making memories together."

Meera: "Absolutely! There's something magical about being out here, away from everything."

Kartik, walking beside Arushi, couldn't agree more. The hike had deepened their connection, and he felt a newfound sense of confidence as they navigated down the trail together.

Arushi: "I love how every step brings us closer to the ground, but it also feels like we're stepping into something new, doesn't it?"

Kartik nodded, his heart racing at her words.

Kartik: "It does. Every moment with you feels like a new adventure."

As they reached the base of the trail, the group found a cozy clearing perfect for camping. The area was surrounded by tall trees, providing a sense of privacy. They set up their tents, Aniket taking charge of the campfire while Meera organized the snacks. The warmth of the fire flickered as the sun set completely, revealing a blanket of stars overhead.*

With the fire crackling, they gathered around, roasting marshmallows and preparing s'mores. The atmosphere was filled with excitement and a hint of nostalgia. Kartik found himself stealing glances at Arushi, who was animatedly sharing a funny story about her childhood. He couldn't help but admire the way the firelight danced in her eyes.

Meera: "Okay, who's ready for some s'mores? I brought the chocolate, the marshmallows, and graham crackers!"

Aniket: "Count me in! You can never go wrong with s'mores after a day of hiking!"

Kartik chuckled, shaking his head in disbelief at how easily they could slip back into their playful banter. He reached for a marshmallow, holding it over the fire.

Arushi: "Just don't burn it, Kartik! You'll ruin the s'more!"

Kartik smirked, looking at her with mock seriousness.

Kartik: "I'll have you know that I'm a marshmallow-roasting expert!"

The group erupted in laughter as he exaggeratedly fanned the marshmallow over the flames. After a moment, he pulled it away, revealing a perfectly golden treat. He carefully assembled the s'more, presenting it to Arushi with a flourish.

Kartik: "Behold! The perfect s'more, made with love!"

Arushi took the s'more, a teasing smile on her face.

Arushi: "Thanks, chef! Let's see if it tastes as good as it looks!"

She took a bite, her eyes lighting up as the chocolate melted in her mouth. Kartik watched her, feeling a swell of joy at her happiness. The warmth of the fire and the laughter of friends created a bubble of comfort around them. As they continued to enjoy their treats, the conversation drifted toward their dreams and aspirations.*

Aniket: "What's everyone's dream destination? If you could go anywhere, where would it be?"

Meera thought for a moment, her eyes sparkling with excitement.

Meera: "I've always wanted to see the Northern Lights! Imagine being under a sky filled with colors!"

Arushi: "That sounds incredible! I'd love to explore the beaches of Bali, soaking up the sun and enjoying the ocean."

Kartik listened, a smile on his face. He knew what his dream destination was—wherever Arushi would be. He decided to share his own thoughts.

Kartik: "I think I'd like to explore the mountains of Switzerland. There's something about the peaks and the snow that calls to me. And maybe... if I'm lucky, I could take a trip with someone special."

He glanced at Arushi, who looked at him with interest.

Arushi: "That sounds amazing, Kartik. I can picture it—the serene beauty of the mountains, a perfect backdrop for an adventure."

The fire crackled, and for a moment, they all fell silent, lost in their thoughts. Then Meera leaned in, her tone playful.

Meera: "So, Kartik, do you have someone special in mind?"

Kartik's heart raced, and he felt a wave of warmth wash over him. He exchanged a quick glance with Arushi, their eyes locking for a moment, and he felt a surge of courage.

Kartik: "Actually, I do. Someone who makes every moment feel special."

Aniket raised an eyebrow, grinning as he caught on to Kartik's meaning.

Aniket: "Ooooh, this is getting interesting! Care to share more?"

Kartik felt his cheeks heat up, but he knew he couldn't shy away from this moment. It was time to be honest, not just with himself but with Arushi as well.

Kartik: "You see, it's someone who brings out the best in me, someone I admire deeply, and... someone I want to get to know even better."

Arushi's breath caught slightly, her expression shifting from playful to serious.

Arushi: "Kartik, I..."

Before she could finish, Aniket interrupted, sensing the moment was turning more serious than he intended.

Aniket: "Alright, enough of this! Let's focus on the stars! Who can name the most constellations?"

Meera rolled her eyes playfully, clearly annoyed at the interruption, but Kartik appreciated Aniket's attempt to lighten the mood. The group shifted gears, their eyes scanning the night sky filled with twinkling stars.*

As they pointed out constellations, Kartik felt a mix of emotions swirling within him. He wanted to tell Arushi how he truly felt, but at the same time, he valued their friendship too much to risk it. The fire crackled, and the laughter continued, but in the back of his mind, the question lingered—was this the right time to express his feelings?

The night wore on, and they shared stories, dreams, and laughter under the stars. Kartik stole glances at Arushi, whose smile illuminated the darkness, and he couldn't help but wonder if she felt the same way he did. As the fire began to fade, the stars became more vibrant, their brilliance filling the night sky.

Kartik: "You know, no matter where we go, as long as we're together, it'll always feel like home."

Arushi turned to him, her expression softening as she met his gaze.

Arushi: "I feel the same way, Kartik. I wouldn't trade these moments for anything."

Kartik's heart raced at her words. He knew this was a moment he wouldn't forget. The connection between them felt undeniable, and he wondered if the stars above were aligning for them in more ways than one.*

CHAPTER THIRTY-NINE

Unspoken Words

As dawn broke, the first light of morning filtered through the trees, casting a golden hue over the campsite. The air was cool, filled with the earthy scent of dew-soaked leaves. The group slowly began to stir, the sounds of birds chirping creating a gentle wake-up call.

Aniket, still half-asleep, stretched out beside the dying embers of the campfire.

Aniket: "Is it morning already? Can't we just sleep for five more minutes?"

Meera, already up and sipping her coffee, grinned mischievously.

Meera: "Come on, sleepyhead! You promised to make breakfast. The early bird gets the worm, remember?"

Kartik, sitting up and rubbing his eyes, chuckled at their playful banter. He turned to see Arushi emerging from her tent, her hair slightly tousled and a bright smile on her face.

Arushi: "Good morning, everyone! Is breakfast ready? I could definitely go for some pancakes."

Kartik felt a warmth spread through him at the sight of her. The previous night had been filled with unspoken words and shared moments, and now, as they gathered around the fire, he was determined to be open about his feelings.

Aniket groaned but finally got up, stretching again before heading toward the food supplies.

Aniket: "Alright, alright! Just for you, Arushi, I'll whip up the best pancakes you've ever had. But you owe me one for making me get up early."

Meera laughed, her eyes sparkling with mischief.

Meera: "How about a back massage after breakfast? That seems fair."

Kartik watched as the friends teased each other, the atmosphere light and joyful. He turned his attention back to Arushi, who was busy organizing the picnic area. He knew today was the day he needed to share his heart. Gathering his courage, he cleared his throat.

Kartik: "Hey, Arushi, can we talk for a moment? Away from the chaos?"

Arushi looked at him, curiosity flickering in her eyes.

Arushi: "Sure! Let's go for a walk."

They walked a short distance into the woods, the trees providing a peaceful backdrop for their conversation. The sounds of laughter faded as they stepped into a quiet clearing, sunlight filtering through the branches. Kartik took a deep breath, feeling both excited and nervous.

Kartik: "So, I've been thinking a lot about everything—the hike, the stars, our friendship..."

Arushi paused, turning to face him. Her expression was serious yet encouraging.

Arushi: "Me too. I felt something special last night. I just didn't know how to say it."

Kartik's heart raced, sensing a moment of truth was upon them. He took a step closer, wanting to bridge the gap between them.

Kartik: "I've realized that what I feel for you goes beyond friendship. You inspire me, Arushi. You make me want to be a better person. I admire your strength, your kindness... everything about you."

Arushi's eyes widened, and for a moment, he thought he saw a glimmer of surprise, followed by a warm smile.

Arushi: "Kartik, I—"

Kartik interrupted, wanting to express everything that had been building inside him.

Kartik: "Let me finish, please. I know we've built something beautiful between us, and I can't keep pretending it's just friendship. I'm ordinary by looks, but I promise I'm extraordinary by heart. And I want to be someone special in your life. Will you be my forever?"

Silence enveloped them, and Kartik's heart pounded in his chest as he awaited her response. Arushi looked taken aback, her eyes reflecting a whirlwind of emotions.

Arushi: "Kartik, I... wow. I didn't expect that, but I feel the same way. I've been scared to admit it, thinking I might ruin what we have."

Kartik felt a wave of relief wash over him, but he held his breath, still unsure.

Arushi: "I've seen how caring and supportive you are, how you see the world differently. It's rare, and it's beautiful. I want to explore this with you."

Kartik's heart soared, and he couldn't help but smile.

Kartik: "So, we're on the same page?"

Arushi laughed softly, her voice filled with joy.

Arushi: "Absolutely! I want to give this a chance, to see where it leads us."

Feeling a mix of happiness and disbelief, Kartik took a step closer, closing the distance between them. For a moment, they simply stood together, the world around them fading as they shared a look filled with promise. The connection they had deepened in the quiet of the woods, and he felt grateful for the moment.

Kartik: "Thank you for being brave enough to embrace this with me. I can't wait to see where our journey takes us."

As they made their way back to the camp, Kartik couldn't help but feel lighter, as if a weight had been lifted from his shoulders. The laughter and chatter from their friends greeted them as they returned, but the bond between him and Arushi felt stronger than ever.

After breakfast, the group decided to embark on another short hike to explore the nearby waterfall, excitedly discussing their plans as they packed their gear. Arushi and Kartik exchanged glances filled with understanding, their hearts echoing with the promise of new beginnings.

Aniket: "Come on, let's see who can get to the waterfall first! Last one there has to do all the dishes tonight!"

Meera: "You're on! I'm ready to race!"

As they set off, Kartik felt a renewed sense of purpose. He had taken a leap of faith, and now he was ready to embrace whatever came next. The forest was alive with the sounds of nature, and every step felt like a celebration of the bond he was beginning to forge with Arushi.

CHAPTER FORTY

A Starlit Confession

The sun dipped below the horizon, painting the sky in hues of orange and purple as the group settled around a small campfire. The warmth of the fire contrasted with the cool evening breeze, wrapping them in a comforting embrace. Kartik watched the flames dance, feeling grateful for the day they had shared.

Aniket broke the peaceful silence, tossing a twig into the fire.

Aniket: "Alright, who wants to share a story? Something funny or embarrassing!"

Meera chimed in, a twinkle in her eye.

Meera: "I have a good one! Remember that time at the company picnic when Aniket tried to impress everyone with his 'expert' grilling skills?"

Kartik laughed, nodding as he remembered the incident.

Kartik: "Oh yes! The burgers were practically charcoal! It was a miracle nobody got sick!"

Aniket feigned indignation.

Aniket: "Hey! I was experimenting! I thought I could impress you all with my culinary talents!"

Arushi leaned in, her eyes sparkling with laughter.

Arushi: "Well, you certainly made an impression, just not the one you were hoping for!"

The laughter echoed through the evening air, creating a joyful atmosphere. As the stories continued, Kartik felt the bonds of friendship deepen. Yet, amid the laughter, his thoughts kept drifting to Arushi. The way her smile lit up the night made his heart race, and he found himself wanting to share something deeper, something more personal.

Finally, after a round of funny stories, the mood shifted, and Meera looked around at her friends.

Meera: "Let's do something different now. How about we each share a dream we have? Something we want to achieve in life?"

Kartik felt a flutter of nervousness at the thought. Would he dare to share his dreams with everyone, especially with Arushi sitting right there? But he saw the sincerity in her eyes, encouraging him to open up.

Aniket nodded, a thoughtful expression on his face.

Aniket: "I like that idea. I'll go first! I dream of starting my own tech company one day, something that can really make a difference. I want to create innovative solutions that help people."

The group cheered, appreciating Aniket's ambition. Meera followed suit, sharing her dream of traveling the world and documenting her adventures through photography.

Meera: "I want to capture the beauty of different cultures and share their stories through my lens. That's what makes life so rich!"

Kartik felt inspired by their dreams and finally found the courage to share his own.

Kartik: "I've always wanted to write a book. Something that resonates with people, maybe a story about overcoming obstacles and finding love. I think everyone has a story worth telling."

The group nodded, and Arushi leaned in closer, her expression genuinely interested.

Arushi: "That sounds amazing, Kartik! What kind of story would it be?"

Kartik felt a warmth spread through him at her encouragement. He took a deep breath, feeling the fire crackle beside them.

Kartik: "It would be about two people from different worlds who learn to see beyond appearances. It's about how real beauty lies in the heart and how love can change everything."

Arushi smiled, her eyes shining with admiration.

Arushi: "That's beautiful, Kartik. I believe your story would inspire so many people."

Encouraged by her words, Kartik continued.

Kartik: "I just want to show that it's okay to be different, to embrace who you are, and to love fiercely. I want people to understand that they're not alone in their struggles."

Aniket clapped his hands together, his face lit up with excitement.

Aniket: "I'd read that book! I'm in! You have to write it!"

The others chimed in, echoing their support. Kartik felt a swell of pride and motivation, especially from Arushi's unwavering encouragement. The moment felt significant, as if he were sharing a piece of himself with them.*

After a few more dreams were shared, the night began to grow quiet, and the stars appeared in the vast sky, twinkling like diamonds. The atmosphere shifted as the group settled back, taking in the beauty of the night. Kartik's heart raced as he felt the moment was right. He turned to Arushi, who was gazing up at the stars, lost in thought.

Kartik: "Arushi?"

She turned her gaze toward him, her expression softening.

Arushi: "Yes, Kartik?"

Kartik swallowed hard, feeling vulnerable yet determined.

Kartik: "Can I share something with you? Something I've been thinking about for a while?"

Arushi nodded, her interest piqued.

Arushi: "Of course! You can share anything with me."

Kartik took a deep breath, trying to find the right words.

Kartik: "I've really enjoyed spending time with you. More than I can express. You make everything feel brighter, and you inspire me to be a better person. I want you to know that my feelings for you have grown deeper."

Arushi's eyes widened slightly, and for a moment, silence enveloped them. The crackling of the fire filled the air as Kartik waited for her response, his heart racing with anticipation.

Arushi: "Kartik, I…"

Before she could finish, Aniket's playful voice interrupted from across the fire.

Aniket: "Hey! Who's up for s'mores? We can't let this beautiful night go to waste!"

The moment broke, and Kartik felt a rush of frustration and hope. Arushi glanced at Aniket, then back at Kartik, her expression a mixture of surprise and amusement.

Kartik (forcing a smile): "Sure, s'mores sound great."

As they all joined in on making s'mores, Kartik couldn't help but feel a mix of emotions—hopeful yet anxious about what he had tried to convey. Despite the interruption, the connection with Arushi felt undeniable, and he was determined to find the right moment again.

The night wore on, filled with laughter and the sweet taste of roasted marshmallows. Kartik stole glances at Arushi, wondering if she had understood his feelings. Deep inside, he felt that this journey was just beginning, and he was ready to explore it, one step at a time.

The Unveiling

The next morning, the group woke up to the sound of birds chirping and the sun peeking through the trees. Kartik felt a mix of excitement and anxiety as they gathered for breakfast. The fire from the previous night still smoldered softly, a reminder of the heartfelt moments shared.

Aniket stretched and grinned, looking at everyone with a spark of energy.

Aniket: "I don't know about you all, but I'm ready for an adventure today! How about a hike up that hill? The view from the top must be incredible!"

Meera clapped her hands in agreement, her enthusiasm infectious.

Meera: "Yes! Let's do it! I want to capture some stunning photos up there!"

Arushi smiled, looking at Kartik, her eyes gleaming with anticipation.

Arushi: "What do you think, Kartik? Are you up for a little hike?"

Kartik nodded, feeling a surge of determination. This was the perfect opportunity to connect with Arushi, and he wanted to make the most of it.

Kartik: "Absolutely! Let's conquer that hill together!"

As they finished their breakfast and prepared for the hike, Kartik felt a rush of determination. This was the moment he had been waiting for, a chance to express his feelings again in a more intimate setting.

The hike began with laughter and friendly banter. Kartik fell into step beside Arushi, his heart racing with every shared glance. Aniket and Meera chatted ahead, while Kartik and Arushi walked together, the conversation flowing easily between them.

Arushi: "I love spending time in nature. It feels so refreshing to escape the city for a while."

Kartik smiled, encouraged by her openness.

Kartik: "I agree. There's something peaceful about being outdoors. It gives me clarity."

As they climbed higher, the trail narrowed, and the trees around them became denser. The atmosphere shifted, and Kartik could feel the energy between him and Arushi intensifying. He decided it was now or never.

Kartik: "Arushi, can we take a quick break up there? I want to show you something."

She raised an eyebrow, intrigued.

Arushi: "Show me what?"

Kartik pointed to a large rock formation up ahead that seemed perfect for resting and enjoying the view.

Kartik: "That spot looks great! I have something I want to discuss, and I'd prefer it to be just us for a moment."

Arushi nodded, her curiosity piqued. They picked up the pace, eager to reach the rock formation. Once there, they settled on the sun-warmed stones, catching their breath and taking in the breathtaking view of the valley below.

Kartik: "Isn't it beautiful?"

Arushi nodded, her eyes sparkling as she gazed at the scenery.

Arushi: "It really is. I could stay here forever."

Kartik shifted slightly, feeling the weight of his heart in his chest. He turned to face her, his expression earnest.

Kartik: "Arushi, there's something I need to tell you. I've been thinking about this for a long time."

She turned to him, her expression serious yet encouraging.

Arushi: "What is it, Kartik? You can tell me anything."

Kartik took a deep breath, gathering his thoughts. This was the moment he had been waiting for, a chance to share his heart with the person who inspired him the most.

Kartik: "Ever since we started spending time together, I've realized how special you are to me. You bring so much light into my life, and I admire your strength and passion."

Arushi's gaze softened, and Kartik continued, his heart pounding.

Kartik: "I know I may not look like the kind of guy who catches attention easily, but I want you to know that I am ordinary by looks, but extraordinary by heart. Will you be my forever?"

The moment hung in the air, charged with emotion. Arushi's eyes widened, surprise and joy mingling in her expression.

Arushi: "Kartik... I..."

Kartik felt his heart race, the silence stretching between them. Had he ruined the moment? He held his breath, waiting for her response. Finally, she smiled, and it felt like the world shifted in that instant.

Arushi: "I feel the same way! I've been waiting for you to say something! Yes, I want to be with you!"

Kartik's heart soared as her words washed over him, filling him with a sense of relief and joy. They shared a beautiful smile, both knowing that this was the beginning of something profound.

Kartik: "Really? You mean it?"

Arushi nodded, her smile radiant.

Arushi: "Absolutely! I've always appreciated your kindness and your heart. You are extraordinary in ways I didn't expect."

In that moment, surrounded by nature and each other, they both felt a warmth spreading through them, a bond formed by genuine connection. Kartik reached for her hand, intertwining their fingers.

Kartik: "Thank you for seeing me, Arushi. I promise to cherish this connection we have."

Arushi squeezed his hand, her expression sincere.

Arushi: "And I promise to be there for you, Kartik. I can't wait to see where this journey takes us."

As they sat together, watching the sun shine on the valley below, they knew this was just the beginning of their story—a beautiful adventure fueled by love, understanding, and endless possibilities.

CHAPTER FORTY-TWO

A Turning Point

The sun began its descent, casting a golden hue over the landscape as Kartik and Arushi continued to enjoy their moment on the rock formation. After a beautiful silence, they decided to head back down the trail. As they made their way, their hands still intertwined, they shared stories and laughter, their bond growing stronger with every step.

Aniket and Meera were waiting for them at the base of the hill, leaning against a tree, their faces curious as they spotted the couple approaching. Aniket raised an eyebrow, a playful grin on his face.

Aniket: "Well, well! Look who's back! Did you two have a romantic heart-to-heart up there?"

Meera nudged him, a knowing smile on her face.

Meera: "Come on, Aniket. Let them have their moment! We're just happy for them!"

Kartik and Arushi exchanged glances, their cheeks flushed with excitement. Arushi took a deep breath, feeling ready to share their news.

Arushi: "Actually, we did! Kartik asked me to be with him, and I said yes!"

Aniket's eyes widened in surprise, followed by a wide grin.

Aniket: "That's amazing! Congrats, you two!"

Meera clapped her hands, her excitement bubbling over.

Meera: "I knew it! You guys are perfect for each other!"

Kartik chuckled, feeling a wave of warmth wash over him. The support from their friends meant everything.

Kartik: "Thanks, guys. It feels surreal, but I couldn't be happier."

As they chatted and celebrated the new relationship, a familiar anxiety crept into Kartik's mind. He loved Arushi deeply, but he couldn't help but wonder if he would be enough for her. As they walked back to the campsite, he decided to voice his thoughts.

Kartik: "Hey, can I ask you something?"

Aniket nodded, intrigued.

Aniket: "Of course! What's on your mind?"

Kartik glanced at Arushi, who was playfully teasing Meera about her photography skills. His heart raced again as he turned back to Aniket.

Kartik: "Do you think I can really be what Arushi deserves? I mean, she's incredible, and sometimes I feel like I'm just... ordinary."

Aniket slapped him on the back, laughter in his voice.

Aniket: "Listen, man, you are more than just your looks. You have a heart of gold, and that's what matters! If Arushi sees that, then she's already chosen wisely. You need to believe in yourself as much as we do."

Kartik felt a flicker of hope, but the doubts still lingered. He glanced at Arushi, who was now taking selfies with Meera, her laughter echoing through the trees.

Meera: "Okay, everyone say 'extraordinary'!"

They all gathered around, striking funny poses, and the camera clicked, capturing their joy. Kartik couldn't help but smile at how effortlessly happy Arushi seemed. But he still felt a weight of insecurity creeping in.

Later that evening, as the group sat around the campfire roasting marshmallows, Kartik felt the need to speak up. The warm glow of the fire illuminated their faces, and he could see the camaraderie and happiness around him. But inside, he wrestled with doubt.

Kartik: "You know, I've always thought that my looks held me back. And now that I'm with Arushi, I worry that I won't be enough for her."

Arushi looked over, her expression shifting to concern.

Arushi: "Kartik, why would you think that? You're everything I've wanted! It's your kindness, your intelligence, and your heart that matter to me."

Meera nodded, chiming in.

Meera: "Exactly! It's not about how you look; it's about who you are inside. You're incredible just as you are."

Kartik took a deep breath, the warmth of their support surrounding him. He knew he had to believe in their words.

Kartik: "I appreciate it, really. I guess I just need to work on my self-esteem. It's hard sometimes, you know?"

Aniket leaned forward, his voice serious yet encouraging.

Aniket: "It's okay to feel that way. We all have insecurities. What's important is how you push through them. You've got a whole team here, supporting you."

As the fire crackled and sparks danced into the night sky, Kartik realized that he wasn't alone in his struggles. With Arushi by his side, and friends who believed in him, he felt a renewed sense of strength.

Kartik: "You guys are right. I need to focus on being the best version of myself for Arushi and for me. I won't let insecurities hold me back."

Arushi smiled brightly, her eyes filled with admiration.

Arushi: "That's the spirit, Kartik! I'm here with you, every step of the way."

The group spent the rest of the evening sharing stories and laughter, the bond between them growing stronger. As the night deepened, Kartik felt a sense of peace wash over him. With his friends and Arushi, he was ready to embrace whatever challenges lay ahead.

The next day brought more adventures. With their spirits high, the group decided to explore a nearby lake. The crystal-clear water sparkled under the sun, and everyone jumped in for a refreshing swim. Kartik and Arushi found themselves floating side by side, the warmth of the sun enveloping them as they enjoyed the moment together.

Kartik: "This is perfect! I couldn't ask for a better day."

Arushi smiled, splashing water playfully at him.

Arushi: "You're right! I love how carefree everything feels right now."

As they floated, Kartik glanced at Arushi, her hair glistening in the sunlight and her laughter filling the air. He couldn't help but feel grateful for this new chapter in his life. He was ready to embrace every moment with Arushi by his side.

Arushi: "Hey, let's make a pact. No matter what happens, we promise to be there for each other. Deal?"

Kartik nodded eagerly.

Kartik: "Deal! I'm in. We'll face everything together."

Their hands met beneath the water, sealing their promise, and in that moment, Kartik knew they were unstoppable. The journey ahead would be filled with challenges, but with Arushi and their friends beside him, he felt ready to take on the world.

As the day unfolded with laughter and adventure, Kartik found himself growing more confident in their relationship. Every shared moment, every laugh, and every challenge made their bond stronger. He was beginning to understand that love wasn't just about being perfect; it was about being real, vulnerable, and supportive of one another.

With this realization, he felt a profound sense of hope for the future. The ripple effect of their connection had just begun, and Kartik couldn't wait to see where it would lead them.

CHAPTER FORTY-THREE

Facing Challenges

The days turned into weeks, and Kartik and Arushi continued to grow closer. They spent their evenings studying together, exploring new hobbies, and simply enjoying each other's company. However, life wasn't without its challenges. With exams approaching, the pressure began to mount. One evening, as they sat in Kartik's living room surrounded by textbooks, he noticed Arushi staring blankly at her notes.

Kartik: "Hey, what's going on? You seem a bit out of it."

Arushi sighed, running her fingers through her hair in frustration.

Arushi: "I don't know, Kartik. I've been feeling overwhelmed lately. The exams are just around the corner, and I'm worried I won't be able to keep up."

Kartik moved closer, concern etched on his face.

Kartik: "You're one of the smartest people I know! You've got this. What part are you struggling with?"

Arushi took a deep breath, her eyes clouding with anxiety.

Arushi: "It's just... I feel like everyone else has it together, and I'm falling behind. What if I don't do well?"

Kartik placed his hand on hers, offering support.

Kartik: "Listen, it's okay to feel this way. We all have our moments of doubt. Remember when we first met? You helped me with my struggles, and now it's my turn to help you."

Arushi smiled faintly, grateful for his reassurance.

Arushi: "You're right. I just need to refocus and stay positive. Let's study together; maybe that will help."

Kartik grinned, the light returning to his eyes.

Kartik: "Absolutely! We'll tackle this together. I'll even bring snacks!"

They dove back into their studies, with Kartik explaining complex concepts and Arushi taking diligent notes. The atmosphere lightened as they joked and shared stories, their bond deepening even further. But as the days went by, Kartik couldn't shake the feeling that Arushi was still carrying a weight on her shoulders. He decided to check in with her again.

A few days later, they took a break from studying and went for a walk in the park. The fresh air felt revitalizing, and Kartik hoped this would lift Arushi's spirits. As they strolled along the path, he finally spoke up.

Kartik: "You know, I've noticed you seem a bit stressed. Is everything okay?"

Arushi paused, looking away for a moment before turning back to him.

Arushi: "I appreciate you asking, Kartik. It's just... I've been feeling this pressure to perform. My parents have high expectations for me, and I don't want to let them down."

Kartik nodded, understanding flooding his mind.

Kartik: "That's a lot to carry. But remember, you're doing this for yourself too. Your happiness matters, not just their expectations."

Arushi sighed, the tension in her shoulders slowly easing.

Arushi: "You're right. I've lost sight of why I started studying in the first place. I love learning; I shouldn't let stress overshadow that."

Kartik smiled, his heart swelling with pride for her.

Kartik: "Exactly! Let's make a deal. For every study session, we'll reward ourselves with something fun afterward. Like ice cream or a movie night. Sound good?"

Arushi laughed, the lightness returning to her spirit.

Arushi: "That sounds perfect! You always know how to cheer me up."

As they continued their walk, they came across a small café with outdoor seating. The scent of freshly brewed coffee wafted through the air, and Kartik suggested they stop for a quick treat.

Kartik: "How about we celebrate our study progress with a little pick-me-up?"

Arushi nodded enthusiastically, and they settled into a cozy corner with their drinks. As they chatted and enjoyed their time together, Arushi felt a wave of gratitude wash over her. Kartik's unwavering support was a comforting anchor amid the storm of expectations.*

The following week, Kartik and Arushi were in the library studying late into the night. Aniket and Meera joined them, creating a small study group. Laughter filled the air as they shared snacks and jokes, creating an atmosphere of camaraderie that lightened the burden of studying.

Aniket: "Alright, everyone! Let's have a quick quiz to see who's been paying attention!"

Kartik: "I'm in! Bring it on!"

Meera rolled her eyes playfully.

Meera: "You guys are ridiculous. But fine, let's do it!"

As the quiz began, Kartik felt a surge of confidence. He answered question after question with ease, and Arushi looked on, impressed. After the quiz, they all celebrated with more snacks and laughter. However, as the night wore on, Kartik noticed Arushi's focus waning again. He leaned closer to her.

Kartik: "You okay? You seem distracted."

Arushi looked down, biting her lip.

Arushi: "I just can't shake this feeling of doubt. What if I still don't do well?"

Kartik squeezed her hand gently.

Kartik: "We're in this together, remember? Just do your best and trust yourself. I believe in you, and I know you'll shine."

Arushi smiled, a flicker of hope igniting within her.

Arushi: "Thanks, Kartik. I really needed to hear that."

As they continued to study, Kartik felt a sense of pride in being there for Arushi, offering her the support she needed. And for the first time in a while, Arushi felt a spark of confidence returning. Together, they were not just studying for exams; they were building a partnership that was rooted in love and mutual support.

❧❧❧

As the exam day approached, Kartik made it a point to encourage Arushi every chance he got. They created a study schedule that balanced hard work with fun breaks, and soon enough, the day of the exam arrived. The atmosphere was tense, but Kartik was determined to keep Arushi calm.

Before they entered the exam hall, Kartik held her shoulders, looking into her eyes.

Kartik: "You're going to do amazing. Just remember to breathe and take your time. I'll be right here waiting for you afterward."

Arushi nodded, a mix of nerves and excitement bubbling within her.

Arushi: "Thanks, Kartik. I really appreciate you being here for me."

With that, they headed into the exam room, ready to face whatever challenges awaited them. Kartik settled into his seat, determined to do his best as well, all the while thinking about how proud he was of Arushi and their growing bond.

After the exam, they reunited outside the hall, where Arushi's face lit up with a mixture of relief and joy.

Arushi: "I think I did well! I felt more confident this time."

Kartik grinned, pulling her into a tight hug.

Kartik: "I knew you could do it! Now, let's celebrate!"

They headed to a nearby café, where they indulged in their favorite desserts, laughter and excitement filling the air. Kartik felt a renewed sense of confidence in himself, too. Being there for Arushi and seeing her succeed inspired him to push past his own doubts. They were building something beautiful together, and he couldn't wait to see where it would lead.

As the days turned into weeks, they continued to support each other through their studies, exams, and everything in between. The challenges they faced only served to strengthen their bond, and Kartik knew that this was just the beginning of their journey together. With love, laughter, and a promise to be there for each other, they were ready to take on the world.

CHAPTER FORTY-FOUR

The Last Step

A cozy café where Kartik and Arushi often meet....

(The café is bustling with chatter and the aroma of fresh coffee fills the air. Kartik sits at a corner table, nervously tapping his fingers on the wooden surface. Arushi arrives, her smile instantly brightening the room.)

Arushi: (sitting down) "Hey! You look like you've seen a ghost. What's on your mind?"

Kartik: (takes a deep breath) "I've been thinking... about everything that's happened between us, and what it means for the future."

Arushi: "Kartik, we've been through a lot. You know I care about you deeply."

Kartik: (nods) "I know. But I feel like there's something important we haven't discussed yet."

(Aniket and Meera walk in, spotting the two at the table. They wave excitedly and join them.)

Aniket: "What's the serious talk about? Did you finally confess your love, Kartik?"

Meera: (teasingly) "Or are you just going to keep us in suspense?"

Kartik: (smiling nervously) "Actually, I was just about to bring up how important our friendship is to me."

Arushi: (gazes at him warmly) "And it's important to me too, Kartik. You mean a lot to me."

Aniket: "So, what's the hold-up? Are we doing this or not?"

Kartik: (looking at Arushi) "I want to take our relationship to the next level. I believe we're ready for that."

Meera: (excitedly) "That sounds amazing! What do you have in mind?"

Kartik: (gathering courage) "I think it's time we truly commit to each other. I want to be there for you, Arushi, in every way possible. I want us to be partners, not just in love but in life."

Arushi: (eyes sparkling) "You really mean that? After everything we've been through?"

Kartik: "Absolutely. I'm not perfect, but I promise to always be there for you."

(Aniket and Meera exchange glances, clearly moved by the moment.)

Aniket: "Well, this is a big step. Are you ready for it, Arushi?"

Meera: "You both have been through a lot together, and it shows how much you care."

Arushi: (takes a deep breath) "I'm ready. I want this, Kartik. I want us."

Kartik: (smiling broadly) "Then let's do this together. I'm ordinary by looks, but I promise I'll always be extraordinary by heart. Will you be my forever?"

(Arushi's smile widens, and she nods.)

Arushi: "Yes, Kartik. Yes! I want to be with you, always."

(The café buzzes around them, but in this moment, it feels like they're in their own world.)

Aniket: "You two are officially the cutest couple I know!"

Meera: "This calls for a celebration!"

(They clink their coffee cups together, laughter filling the air as they toast to new beginnings.)

(As the scene fades, Kartik and Arushi share a knowing look, ready to face whatever comes next, hand in hand.)

CHAPTER FORTY-FIVE

The Journey

(Kartik and Arushi walk side by side, hands intertwined, soaking in the beauty around them.)

Kartik: (looking at the sunset) "Isn't this beautiful? Just like us, starting anew."

Arushi: (squeezing his hand) "It truly is. I've never felt this happy before. It's like everything has fallen into place."

Kartik: "I've realized that it's not just about us. It's about what we can create together, the lives we can touch."

(Aniket and Meera join them, bringing a picnic basket.)

Aniket: "Look what we brought! It's time to celebrate your new chapter, lovebirds!"

Meera: (setting up the blanket) "And of course, to remind you both how lucky you are to have each other!"

Kartik: (laughing) "You two are incredible. Thank you for always supporting us."

(They all sit down, enjoying the snacks and each other's company. The atmosphere is filled with laughter and playful teasing.)

Meera: "So, what's the first thing you want to do as a couple?"

Arushi: (thoughtfully) "I think we should travel somewhere, just the two of us. A new adventure awaits!"

Kartik: "That sounds perfect! I'd love to explore the mountains with you."

Aniket: "Make sure to take lots of pictures. I want to see all the beautiful places you'll visit."

Meera: "And don't forget to bring me back a souvenir!"

(Laughter erupts as they enjoy the food and each other's company. As the sun sets, the sky becomes a tapestry of colors, reflecting the warmth of their friendship and newfound love.)

Kartik: (taking a moment) "You know, I've been thinking about how we can give back to the community. We've been so blessed with love and friendship."

Arushi: (nodding) "That's a great idea, Kartik. We could volunteer together or start a project that helps others."

Aniket: "Count me in! We can make a real difference together."

Meera: "Absolutely! Let's channel all this positivity into something meaningful."

(The four of them brainstorm ideas, excited about the possibilities that lie ahead.)

Kartik: "It's incredible how much can change in such a short time. I'm grateful for all of you."

Arushi: (leaning her head on Kartik's shoulder) "And I'm grateful for the journey that brought us here."

(The atmosphere grows contemplative as they reflect on their experiences and the challenges they've overcome.)

Aniket: "Remember the times we struggled, the ups and downs? They only made us stronger."

Meera: "And they brought us closer. We're like a family now."

Kartik: "Exactly. And this is just the beginning. We have so much more to experience, together."

(As the last rays of sunlight fade, they sit in comfortable silence, their hearts full of hope and anticipation for what lies ahead.)

(The scene shifts to a montage of their lives over the next few months: Kartik and Arushi exploring new places, volunteering in the community, and growing deeper in love. Aniket and Meera are always by their side, supporting their journey.)

(Finally, the screen fades to black with the words: "And so, their adventure began, not just as a couple but as partners in making the

world a better place, proving that love and friendship can change
lives.")

CHAPTER FORTY-SIX

A Love Beyond Appearances

Kartik and Arushi stand on the balcony, the evening breeze gently rustling their hair. The sky is painted with hues of orange and pink as the sun sets, creating a perfect backdrop for this moment.

Kartik takes a deep breath, his heart racing. He turns to Arushi, who looks radiant in the soft twilight.

Kartik: "Arushi, I've spent so much time doubting myself. I always thought that my looks would define my worth. But you... you showed me that it's my heart that truly matters."

Arushi smiles, her eyes sparkling with understanding.

Arushi: "Kartik, you are so much more than what meets the eye. You've always been there for me, supporting me in ways I never knew I needed. Your kindness and depth are what draw me to you."

He takes a step closer, his heart pounding.

Kartik: "In this journey we've shared, I've learned that love isn't about appearances; it's about connection and understanding. I want you to know that **I am ordinary by looks, extraordinary by heart: will you be my forever?**"

A moment of silence hangs in the air, thick with anticipation. Arushi's breath catches in her throat as she processes his words. Her heart swells with emotion, tears glistening in her eyes.

Arushi: "Yes, Kartik! A thousand times, yes! You are extraordinary in every way that truly matters."

Kartik smiles, relief flooding over him as they embrace, sealing their promise to one another. The sunset transforms into a starry night, symbolizing the beginning of their new journey together.

Meera and Aniket arrive just in time, their faces lit up with joy.

Meera: "What's this? A celebration without us? We heard some serious love declarations!"

Aniket laughs, slapping Kartik on the back.

Aniket: "Told you! She's the one for you, man. Now let's celebrate this moment!"

They all share laughter and joy, surrounded by friends who have been there through thick and thin. As they toast to love, friendship, and new beginnings, Kartik and Arushi glance at each other, knowing their love story is just beginning.

With hearts full of hope and dreams for the future, they embark on a journey together, hand in hand, ready to face whatever life throws at them.

CHAPTER FORTY-SEVEN

A New Dawn

The celebration continued, laughter echoing through the evening air. Kartik and Arushi, still wrapped in each other's embrace, felt as if the world around them had faded away. The stars began to twinkle above, illuminating the path they had chosen together.

As the four friends gathered around the balcony, the atmosphere was filled with warmth and happiness. Aniket raised his glass, his eyes sparkling with mischief.

Aniket: "To Kartik and Arushi! May your love be as deep as the ocean and as bright as the stars!"

Meera chimed in, her voice cheerful: "And to all the adventures yet to come! I can't wait to see what life has in store for you two."

Kartik took a moment to soak in the scene. Surrounded by the people who had supported them, he felt a wave of gratitude wash over him.

Kartik: "Thank you, everyone. Your friendship means the world to us. We couldn't have reached this moment without your love and support."

Arushi squeezed his hand, her heart swelling with joy. She turned to her friends, her voice filled with sincerity.

Arushi: "You all have been our pillars of strength. It's not just about us; it's about this beautiful bond we share. We promise to cherish every moment together."

The evening continued with stories, laughter, and a few playful jabs as they reminisced about the journey that had brought them to this point. As the stars twinkled above, Kartik felt a sense of calm wash over him, knowing that he had finally embraced who he was.

Later that night, as they walked along the balcony, the cool breeze felt refreshing against their skin. Arushi leaned against the railing, her gaze lost in the starlit sky.

Arushi: "Kartik, can you believe how far we've come? From being just friends to this... it feels surreal."

Kartik joined her, wrapping his arm around her shoulders.

Kartik: "I know! I never imagined I could feel this way about someone. You've opened my heart in ways I never thought possible."

Arushi looked up at him, her eyes shimmering with emotion.

Arushi: "And you've shown me what it means to love deeply. I feel safe with you, like I can be my true self without fear."

Kartik turned to face her, his expression serious yet tender.

Kartik: "I want to spend every moment with you, Arushi. I want to create a life filled with love, laughter, and understanding. Together, we can overcome anything."

Arushi nodded, her heart racing at the thought of their future.

Arushi: "Together, we will navigate this journey. I believe in us, in our love."

Just then, Meera and Aniket appeared, breaking the moment with their playful banter.

Meera: "Hey, lovebirds! Enough of the mushy stuff! Let's make some plans for our next adventure!"

Aniket chimed in, grinning: "Yeah, we need to find out if Kartik is really as extraordinary as he claims when it comes to hiking!"

The group burst into laughter, and Kartik felt the warmth of friendship envelop him once again.

Kartik: "Bring it on! I'll show you guys what I'm made of!"

As the night wore on, they shared stories of their dreams and aspirations, their laughter echoing into the night. Each moment was a thread woven into the tapestry of their lives, strengthening their bond.

As the clock struck midnight, Kartik and Arushi found themselves alone again, the world around them silent.

Kartik: "This is just the beginning, isn't it?"

Arushi: "Yes, it is. A beautiful beginning."

With that, they turned to face the horizon, where the first light of dawn began to break. The promise of a new day, filled with endless possibilities, stretched out before them. Hand in hand, they stepped forward, ready to embrace whatever lay ahead, knowing they would face it together.

And in that moment, surrounded by friends and love, Kartik felt extraordinary—not just because of Arushi, but because he had finally learned to embrace his true self.

Epilogue

Years had passed since that fateful day when Kartik and Arushi first dared to express their feelings for one another. The bustling city around them had continued to thrive, yet within the cocoon of their love, time seemed to stand still.

Kartik stood by the window of their cozy apartment, watching as the sun dipped below the horizon, painting the sky in hues of orange and pink. He turned to see Arushi, sitting on the couch with a book in her hands, a soft smile gracing her lips. It was moments like these that filled his heart with gratitude, reminding him of the journey they had traveled together.

"Remember our first coffee date?" Arushi asked, looking up from her book, her eyes sparkling with warmth.

Kartik chuckled, shaking his head. "How could I forget? You ordered that fancy drink, and I just went with a plain black coffee, trying to impress you."

Arushi laughed, her eyes twinkling with mischief. "And you were so nervous you almost spilled it all over yourself!"

"Yeah, I thought I was going to mess it up," he replied, walking over to join her on the couch. "But I didn't realize then that the most beautiful moments often come from being our true selves, without pretense."

Arushi nodded, leaning her head against his shoulder. "It's amazing how far we've come. We've built a life together that I once only dreamed of. I wouldn't trade it for anything."

As they sat in comfortable silence, Kartik felt a wave of emotion wash over him. The insecurities that had once clouded his mind faded into the background, replaced by the unwavering support and love they had cultivated.

"I often think about how we met, how we each had our own battles," Kartik said, breaking the silence. "But together, we became stronger, didn't we?"

"Absolutely," Arushi replied, intertwining her fingers with his. "You taught me to look beyond appearances and embrace what really matters. You're extraordinary, Kartik. Not just to me, but to everyone who knows you."

With a soft smile, Kartik brushed a strand of hair behind Arushi's ear. "And you taught me that love is about connection and understanding. You saw me for who I really am."

They sat together, sharing stories and laughter, as the world outside continued its relentless pace. Their journey was not without challenges, but each obstacle only deepened their bond, reinforcing the belief that true love is not merely a fairy tale; it is a daily choice to choose one another, flaws and all.

In the years to come, Kartik and Arushi would continue to inspire those around them, reminding everyone that beauty lies in authenticity, and the heart's desires are worth pursuing. Together, they ventured into the future, hand in hand, ready to face whatever life had in store, knowing they had found in each other their forever.

As the night fell and the stars began to twinkle in the sky, Kartik whispered, "I am ordinary by looks, but extraordinary by heart. And with you, Arushi, I have discovered the true meaning of love."

Arushi smiled back, her heart full. "And I choose you, today and always."

Thanks For Reading

Dear Reader,

Thank you from the bottom of my heart for taking the time to journey with me through the story of Kartik and Arushi. Their path, filled with self-discovery, love, and the realization that true worth lies beyond appearances, was written with the hope that it would resonate with you on a deeper level. I hope their story sparked inspiration, brought moments of reflection, and reminded you that real beauty, strength, and love come from within.

As you close this book, I invite you to carry the essence of this story with you. Cherish the connections you make, embrace the extraordinary in the everyday, and above all, remain true to who you are. Life is filled with moments—some small, some grand—that define us, and it is in these moments that we discover the true depth of our hearts.

Your support and encouragement mean the world to me. It fuels my passion to write, to share stories, and to continue exploring the themes of love, identity, and the beauty of the human spirit. I hope this book has left you with a sense of hope, warmth, and optimism for the journeys ahead in your own life.

I am excited to share more stories with you in the future. Until then, remember—no matter what life brings, you are extraordinary just as you are.

With deepest gratitude,
Manoj Yadav

About The Author

Manoj Yadav

Manoj Yadav is an accomplished author, motivational speaker, and dedicated storyteller who believes in the transformative power of love and inner strength. With a passion for inspiring others, Manoj writes stories that explore the depths of human emotions and the importance of looking beyond the surface.

His literary journey began with the publication of **It Started with a WhatsApp Message** and continued with **When I Was in**

College, showcasing his ability to weave relatable characters and heartfelt narratives. Each story he tells reflects his commitment to authenticity and connection, drawing readers into worlds where they can see themselves.

In addition to his writing, Manoj is the founder of the MM Foundation tied up with UNICEF India, an NGO dedicated to uplifting individuals and communities through various social initiatives. His mission is to create positive change and empower others to recognize their worth and potential.

Manoj is also the creator of MM Motivation, a platform where he shares motivational insights and life lessons to inspire others. Through daily quotes and engaging content, he encourages individuals to believe in themselves and strive for their dreams.

Join Manoj on his journey as he continues to inspire and uplift through his words, inviting readers to explore the extraordinary within the ordinary.

Instagram.com/manojyadavofficial

Facebook.com/writermanojyadav

Notes

Notes

Notes

Notes

Notes

Notes

Notes